Twisted Death

A Campus Killer

Twisted Death

A Campus Killer

G.L. Barbour

ARPress
45 Dan Road Suite 5
Canton MA 02021

Hotline: 1(888) 821-0229
Fax: 1(508) 545-7580

Ordering Information:
Quantity sales. Special discounts are available on quantity purchases by corporations, associations, and others. For details, contact the publisher at the address above.

Printed in the United States of America.
ISBN-13:   Paperback   979-8-89356-518-8
                eBook   979-8-89356-520-1
                Hardback   979-8-89356-519-5

Library of Congress Control Number: 2024902472

Other Books by G. L. Barbour

<u>Academic</u>

Quality in the Veterans Health Administration
Redefining a Public Health System

<u>Fiction</u>

The Ron Looney Series

Death Unexpected
One, Two, Three Times a Murder
A Researched Death
Naked Death
Alibi for Death

<u>Other</u>

Montana in the Rearview Mirror

Contents

PROLOGUE

The apartment was small, almost cozy. A one-bedroom place, it had matching tiny living area and an eat-in kitchen. The presence of the four men seated around the table seemed to occupy most of the space available. One of the men was older, looked nearly sixty, and had brown hair streaked with broad-brush strokes of yellowish gray. He wore half-glasses perched on a broad and bulbous nose and the eyes behind the frames were small and sharp. He directed a question at the man across the table from him, "This place is good for how long?"

"No mor'n a week," said the man. He was thin and wiry with a rather plain face; his eyes did not actually look at the questioner but generally in his direction. He wore an over-sized V-neck sweater with sleeves pushed up and which kept falling down.

"Then we need a new place for next week," said the older man, clearly the leader of the group. He looked at the men to each side and they nodded.

"I think I'll have a place by then," said the man on the right. He was a large man, close to 300 pounds wearing a sweat stained undershirt. He had a shaved head glistening with sweat and multiple tattoos visible on his large, bare arms. "Looks like the place next door to me is gonna open up in the next day or so."

Satisfied, the leader turned his attention back to the several stacks of money on the table. In front of him was a clipboard to use for tallies.

The other three were counting the money, bundling packets of $1000 and stacking them for his tally. The tabletop held several loose bills and three handguns. The men did their work in silence.

Suddenly, there was a bump at the door and it opened to admit a young woman. Her presence so startled the men that two of them had grabbed their weapons before realizing the absence of any threat. She was carrying a pizza box and a wide-eyed stare that took in the money and the guns.

"Peg," said the wiry man as he stood and positioned himself between the girl and the table. "What're you going here?"

"Ummm. I thought we could watch a movie?" she said hesitatingly.

" I probably should have told you we'd do that some other time," he said starting to move her toward the door.

Behind him the leader had swept most of the money into a duffel bag. He stood and noted that the weapons were concealed. "Look, TJ, we have pretty much finished the count. Don't let us interrupt your date," he said with a light inflection on the idea of a 'date'.

The man called TJ turned questioningly toward the leader who explained, "All we have left to do is to justify the last of these receipts and we'll be outta your hair. Why don't you and the lady go on and watch your movie?" He indicated with his head in the direction of the bedroom where the only television was kept. "I'm sorry we ran over so late."

TJ took the hint and smiled at the girl, "Sure. Good idea." He led her toward the bedroom and locked eyes with the leader as he passed.

CHAPTER 1

In the end, no one was satisfied. The protest marchers wanted a bigger venue and the police wanted less territory to cover. The final agreement on the Special Event Permit issued by the Cincinnati Police Department limited the protesters to a four-block area adjacent to the Hamilton County Courthouse. Between East Central Parkway and E. 9th Street they were allowed to gather and demonstrate on both sides of E. Court Street and on the section of Main Street from the Parkway to 9th. The time of the 'official' protest was from 5:00PM to 10:00 PM but the involved personnel began arriving in the area well before the starting time.

Police officers, in full uniform gathered along the march route on E. Court with large ropes strung along the sidewalks to prevent any approach to the buildings. Officers stood every few feet holding the rope. Other officers, unencumbered by the rope gathered close to the intersections.

Like their counterparts, the protesters also gathered early. They came in from the side streets carrying large banners and individual placards with a variety of abusive and foul language on them. Some wore masks but many did not and all seemed to be carrying something, a bat, a stick, a garden hoe. As their numbers increased, they became more agitated and shouted at the police, screaming epithets they did not learn at the dinner table. Several times the crowd surged toward the retraining rope but did not pass.

Shortly before the 'official' start time two men showed up with bullhorns and began to stir emotions in the crowd by chanting disgusting ditties about police and the degree to which they found them disgusting and reprehensible. The police officers on the restraining line appeared unaffected and did not respond.

A young appearing man suddenly burst through the restraining line and approached one of the buildings with a spray can in his hand. Almost before he had taken the top off the can, officers from the nearest intersection arrived and intercepted him. He was quickly detained, handcuffed and taken away from the gathering. Many of those in the protest crowd who saw what happened hurled further invective at the police, threw bottles and rocks at the officers, and again tried to break through the rope line. They were unsuccessful and ultimately were pushed back to the street.

The bullhorns began to synchronize the crowd's message and the protesters faced eastward toward the county courthouse and began another series of scripted chants raising complaints about police brutality, 'white privilege' in the court system and their belief that the system was 'rigged against people of color'. As the marchers moved eastward another young man broke ranks and ran toward the courthouse with spray can aloft. He was also quickly and easily intercepted, cuffed and removed from the area. The crowd responded with louder chanting and throwing bottles at the officers but no one else tried to break through the restraining line.

Television and newspaper coverage was widespread. Reporters and cameramen were at every intersection and standing on the steps of the courthouse to catch all the action and record the visual and auditory insults from the crowd. Broadcast coverage emphasized the complaints of the crowd: people of color were being treated unfairly and inappropriately by the police. Only the police officers on the line appeared to notice that the crowd was principally composed of white individuals and those were mostly individuals in their 20s. Television cameras did not feature the signs with misspelled words and reporters did not comment on the makeup of the crowd, ignoring the facts of predominant white youth.

Shortly before 10:00 PM police vehicles appeared at the ends of Main Street near the courthouse and the loudspeaker system announced that the official protest would end promptly at 10:00. Stragglers remaining in the area were warned they would be at risk of being arrested for unlawful gathering. This announcement was greeted by jeers and raised fists from the protesters but many immediately began melting away from the area. The protest was completely defused and disbanded by 10:15. A few people had been injured by the mob moving toward the courthouse but not seriously. The police presence began to also leave the area and by midnight the only evidence of the protest was the scattered debris of paper, cans, placards and drink cans littering Court Street.

CHAPTER 2

Arne Thorason came out of his office and looked around the Dick Pen. Arne was the Captain of the Homicide Division of the Cincinnati Police Department and his detectives' offices were located on the fourth floor of the police building in downtown Cincinnati. The offices were clustered in the southwest corner of the floor and were referred to as the 'Dick Pen'. The Captain's office was on the outside corner, closed off from the rest of the open space by flimsy plaster walls surmounted with opaque glass extending to the ceiling. A door shielded the office with frosted glass on which was inscribed "Arne Thorason, Captain, Chief of Detectives".

The Captain was a squarish man, almost six feet tall who seemed at times to be almost that wide. He was a little over 230 pounds and generally comported himself as he did when he was a college linebacker. "Thor" as he was referred to by nearly everyone in the Department had an outstanding career in Homicide and was the natural choice for Captain when that position became available. Truth was, Arne Thorason was more than a little uncomfortable telling seasoned men what the components of their job were or how to do them. Nonetheless, he had accepted the job almost two decades previously and had then undertaken a slow and steady replacement of detectives to get exactly the ones he wanted working with him in the Dick Pen.

Part of Thor's career development strategy was "The Look". When a particular detective found that his work product or the effort he was expending was found lacking in Thor's eyes, he or she shortly came to suffer The Look. It all began with they eyes, the eyes of a middle linebacker fixing a unsuccessful running back as target and putting him down, hard. Whenever Thor squared up, tucked his head and fixed someone with that wide-eyed stare, anyone who could get out of the way would promptly leave the vicinity. After only a few months of this strategy, several individuals requested transfer out of Homicide, creating openings within the division.

Arne Thorason personally interviewed anyone wanting to transfer in and was shortly able to fill available posts in the division with individuals who met his standard. That standard was never expressly stated but everyone understood it was 'start fast and speed up'. Plus, the underlying tenants were also assumed to be, 'don't ask me how to do your job' and 'be successful'. Anyone who could stick to those basic principles would be successful in Homicide. The standard came with a package of trust from Thor, a willingness to allow his detectives fairly broad lanes of scrutiny. He trusted his officers and let them use their intuition and 'gut' feelings rather than expecting strict by-the-book investigation.

The Captain resembled an old time newspaper editor in a jacketless three-piece suit with collar and tie loosened and sleeves rolled up. His eyes went rubbering around the room and found who he was looking for. "Hey, Walker."

"Yes, sir?"

"Got a DB on the University campus," Thorason said, flatly. He continued, somewhat unnecessarily, "You're up."

"Yep," said the target of his comment, Ron Looney, Detective Two in the Homicide Division. Ron was not about to incite 'The Look' and he quickly agreed to the comment and its connotation. Ron had become known in the Department as 'Walker' from his early days in patrol for his propensity to walk the area to which he was assigned rather than cruise in a car. He had spent that time talking with people and becoming known for more than the uniform he wore. 'Walker' Looney was a ten-year veteran of the Homicide Division.

He was also a veteran of the U.S. Air Force military police corps and had spent more than ten of his years in service as a criminal investigator.

His superior officers in the military recognized how Looney used his Arkansas background to recognize behavior patterns and watched him apply plain old common sense to crack several tough cases. They also recognized his complete lack of interest in command. Ron Looney wanted to do the job, not direct others to do it. He was, therefore, a perfect match for Arne Thorason's Homicide Division.

Looney's brother-in-law, who worked in Robbery Division, had recommended him to the Cincinnati Police Department when he retired from the Air Force fourteen years before. It was a good match and Ron had quickly risen in the departmental ranks. When appropriate, he applied for transfer to Homicide and Ron 'Walker' Looney was now happily at a level of activity that he enjoyed and which he did well.

"Address?" he asked as he waved at his partner, Gene Novalchek, who was walking toward their desks holding a Styrofoam cup and making a distasteful face. Gene tossed the cup and its contents into the wastebasket and joined him. Then the two of them headed down the stairs to the garage. The pair was not totally dissimilar. Looney was just under six feet tall, dark of hair, clean shaven and wide of chest, pushing 180 pounds. Novalchek favored his Nordic mother's side being six feet tall and 190 pounds topped by blond hair kept trimmed at a medium level surrounding a boyish face that seemed to have a perpetual smile. But his face was not smiling as he followed Looney to the stairwell.

Halfway down the stairs he turned partially toward his partner without halting his downward progress and asked, "Coffee to go? That rank stuff in the pot up there would take paint off a barn."

"We need to. I haven't had a second cup yet," came the answer.

So, instead of entering the garage when they reached the street, they walked another block and got 'travel cups' at the small coffee shop down the block commonly frequented by officers. There was no line at the counter and they were each able to order, pay and get out of the shop with little wasted motion.

Ron and Gene had been partners for seven years. Ron often felt he had won the lottery on partners. Gene was smart, personable and generally a happy guy. He was noted for quick one-liners and telling funny jokes. Ron thought he could not have persisted in the job if he had been partnered with some of the other detectives in the division. All the detectives were serious and good at their job but they were not, individually, light-hearted like Gene. Nance, for instance, complained about everything and Jim-Bob spent far too much time talking about extraneous things. This moniker was given to two detectives paired because of their southern origins, both from Alabama, one was named James and the other was Robert. Very few people knew which was which and both answered to the 'dual name. Rocky was always expecting that the world was going to end. Each of the other detectives in Homicide had some trait that Ron, who generally preferred working alone, would have found irritating over time. But he enjoyed his work with Gene, even though that meant a daily semi-serious string of complaints about Ron's car.

As they started back to the garage after getting their coffee, Gene raised a common refrain, "We aren't taking your car are we? I'd rather walk than ride shotgun in that bucket."

"We are and you can if you wish," Ron replied.

"C'mon, man. Can't we get an unmarked? They at least have springs."

"Nope. I don't like driving someone else's car. And I'm driving."

"Did you at least get a new suspension?"

"Of course not, Gene. Car doesn't need it."

"I think you'd change your mind if you rode shotgun."

"Clearly not going to happen in my car."

"Pity."

The complaints didn't really cease after entering the car and leaving the garage. Ron was aware this conversation was an over-edited replay of multiple conversations they had in the past. His own responses were nearly automatic but he did wonder what Gene would talk about - or complain about - if they ever did take an unmarked police car.

CHAPTER 3

Looney drove out of the parking garage and turned onto W. Court. He followed Court over several blocks eastward to Vine and then headed north. Gene made a few disparaging comments about the comfort of his seat but mostly the trip was quiet, each man with his own thoughts - and coffee. As partners, they shared thoughts and ideas about crime scenes and the possible felons but they had a practice of each gathering their own information before sharing. They had no information at this time and so had nothing to share.

They transitioned from Vine to Jefferson at the southeast corner of the University grounds and Looney slowed to find the appropriate cross street. Gene looked at Waze on his phone and suggested a left on Daniels and a right on Commons Way. They pulled into parking on the right side of Commons Way just short of the circle intersection with West University. Across the street the small area of greenery marked off with yellow crime scene tape was evident. The detectives got out of the car and approached the uniformed officer at the sidewalk.

As the officer recognized them and went to hold the tape up for them to cross into the crime scene area, Ron asked, "What do we have here?"

"Female student, we think. Broken neck. Sgt. Nichols has more details."

"Thanks," they each said and followed the walkway a few more yards. They encountered another set of tapes surrounding a picnic table in the center of the larger space and Sgt. Nichols talking to the Medical Examiner, Kathryn Darringer. The M.E. looked up and said,

"Good morning boys. Glad to see you had time for coffee."

"We thought there might be blood and gore all over the place," Gene responded. "We needed to settle our stomachs."

"You are always 'settling' your stomach, Detective Novalchek," she fired back. "What did it take this time? Honey bun?"

"Just coffee with cream, Sweetheart", Gene responded, drawing a frown from both his partner and Darringer.

"What?" Gene said, "She called me 'Honey bun."

Darringer shook her head at the absurdity of Gene's comment, turned to look at Ron. "Walker," she nodded to him.

"Doc. What do we have here?" Looney asked.

"Young woman, probably in her twenties. Killed by broken neck without evidence of external trauma."

"You mean no bruising or evidence of having fallen."

"I mean no evidence of any external cause."

"Defensive wounds?"

"None that I can see here."

"Sexual assault?"

"That will have to wait 'til I get her back to the Lab."

Kathryn Darringer, long-time Cincinnati Medical Examiner was wearing her usual blue paper gown with the elastic bands at the wrists and she had covered her feet with surgical booties. She had on a surgical cap and a clear plastic face guard with the plastic shield lifted in front of her face.

Gene took in the incongruity of her dress and the absence of body fluids at the scene. He asked, "Say, Doc, what time is your next jousting duel? I'd like to be there?"

He was answered by an unsmiling stare and the comment, "As I said, you will have to wait - duel or not - until I have her back in my Lab."

Ron was always struck by the Medical Examiner's reference to her work area as 'the Laboratory'; everyone else in the department called it 'the morgue'. Even though the area was one and the same, he admired Darringer for constantly approaching her work as an academic study and not simply as a short-term repository for the dead on their way to a cemetery. Furthermore, Kathryn Darringer had been in her post now for about 18 years and clearly knew what she was doing; she earned a nickname of "Straight-Shooter" as a play on her name and the many times she had reported a key finding that led to an arrest. Darringer had neither endorsed the nickname nor refused it but she always answered promptly when addressed as "Doc."

Looney turned to the Sgt. and asked, "Who found her?"

"A student cutting through on his way to class."

"He still around?"

"Oh yeah. He has no interest in class now. He's over there," the Sgt. said pointing at a young man in cutoffs and polo shirt sitting on another bench with his head bent and his hands on his knees. He had the appearance of someone who was about to vomit - or someone who recently had. He looked up as the detectives approached.

"Are you the one that found her?" Ron asked.

"Yes sir."

"And your name is?"

"Andy. Andy Bucholtz."

"Tell me about finding her, Andy," Ron said in his most friendly voice.

"I was on my way to class . ."

"Where?" interrupted Gene.

"In the Chem Building," he said, waving his arm in the general direction of the buildings behind him.

"Go on," Ron said as if the interruption had not occurred.

"And I cut through the area here and saw her laying on the table." At the memory, Andy swallowed hard and Ron thought he might vomit again.

"Laying on the table?" Looney asked, pushing Andy to remain involved in the questioning.

"Well, she was sitting and had her head down like she was sleeping."

"I see."

"And I tried to wake her up." More hard swallowing accompanied by some deep breaths.

Gene re-entered the conversation, "Why?

"Huh?"

"Why did you try to wake her up? Do you know her?"

"No. I mean I thought she was going to miss class and, uh …"

"So you do know she is a student here?"

"No. I mean why else would she be napping here on campus?"

The detectives looked at Andy for a few seconds, but he just shrugged his shoulders

Ron pressed, " So, you went to awaken her and . . ?"

"And she was all stiff and cold. I called 9-1-1 but I was pretty sure she was dead." Andy made this assertion with only a hint of the nausea from before.

"Did you see anyone else around?" Ron asked, certain in his own mind that no one involved in the killing would have waited around to be seen when rigor set in.

"No. I didn't see anybody till the ambulance arrived."

"Did you touch anything other than touching her to wake her?" Gene asked.

Andy looked at him and briskly shook his head. Gene was fairly certain this student had neither touched anything nor had any interest in the site.

After a few more questions determining that Andy did not know the girl, the detectives went back to the crime scene. The M.E. was impatiently waiting for them to clear the scene so she could take the body back to her 'laboratory'.

"How much longer, boys?" she asked, implying the detectives wee just playing around and delaying the important work she had in front of her.

"Not long, Doc, I promise," Ron said, wryly.

The body still positioned as if asleep, sitting at the table. Each detective walked completely around the table, one clockwise and the other counter-clockwise before coming together for a quick consult. Ron had been working in homicide for several years, growing up in Arkansas he regularly hunted for deer and ducks. The presence of a dead body was not personally disturbing to him; at least a fresh body like this one was not. The floaters and the week-old ones were disturbing but only because of their unnatural appearance and smell.

At the same time Ron usually had an odd feeling at the first approach to a dead person. Very different from approaching a dead animal. In Ron's world, people should be upright and there was something about the usual horizontal position of dead bodies that seemed to tilt the world. This body wasn't horizontal, however. It was sitting, slumped against the table and could very well have been a person sleeping. Still, the world was not right and this body's position was only a part of it.

"Your opinion?" Ron asked his partner.

"If this is the position in which she was found, I'd say she knew the killer and allowed him to put his hands on her."

"Unless she was sleeping and the guy snuck up on her."

Gene paused at this suggestion before asking, "And then what?"

"Well," Ron said too slowly, "then he sneaks up behind her and kills her."

"I don't like that. No motive."

"Well, not one we are aware of, at least. So, yeah, I agree. Probably a known assailant, probably intimate. Anything else?" Ron came away from his suggestion as testing the hypothesis.

"Probably early AM."

"Doc will give us a time. What do you think of the method?"

"Harsh. Especially for someone known intimately. What are you thinking?"

Ron paused a moment, then said quietly, "I think we need to have the doc tell us more about the cause of death."

"Because. . . ?"

"Seems to have been too quick for an average perp. There are no defensive wounds, so the critical attack had to be very quick. I'm thinking more than ordinary strength here."

Gene looked at the body for confirmation of this charge; finding none he nodded to Ron and said, "If you say so."

"I do. At least right now. Things might change after the doc finishes her work."

They signaled for the M.E. to have her technicians collect the body and after that was done they closely examined the area around the body's former position. There were no clues to be found. The area was paved and no footprints were left; there were no items under the body or the table or in the immediate area.

As the technicians were wheeling their gurney with the body back to the M.E.'s wagon, Ron turned back to Sgt. Nichols, "Did you find any identification?"

"Not a whit. Pockets empty. No engraved jewelry. Nothing."

"Well, that's where we will have to start, then. And try to figure out why she was left here. Is she even a student?"

Nichols was a long-timer in the department and was hoping to make detective; he was eager to help. "Don't know. She looks about the right age. How can I help you figure that out?"

"Leave a couple of officers here to question anyone who comes around showing interest. And send someone to the Campus Police to see if anyone has been reported missing."

"Got it."

"Meanwhile we're going to the morgue to get a good picture and then we'll start with the Registrar."

Gene said, "You know those morgue pictures make people look dead, right?"

Ron looked at his partner for a long second before commenting, "Well, Gene, they are dead."

"You know what I mean."

"Yeah, but fortunately our picture won't be taken in the morgue - we will have our picture taken in the Laboratory."

The detectives headed back to Looney's car and Sgt. Nichols pulled the others patrols together for briefing about assignment.

CHAPTER 4

T he young woman's body was just being washed prior to the beginning of the autopsy. Dr. Darringer had meticulous examined her, combed through her hair and pubic region and finished the rape kit examination before. Now while the diener washed the body, she sat at the small worktable near the corner of the room and completed the paperwork. She dictated her notes from the scene and listed the findings and pertinent negatives from her external exam and was just finishing up when the detectives arrived.

Ron noticed the diener finishing the washing and said, "Are we too early or just right, Doc?"

"Depends on what you are interested in," Darringer replied

"Actually all we need at the moment is a good photograph for identification. Are you going to do the post right away?"

"Yes, I am. But you can get your photo first."

The diener helped prop up the woman's body so the Looney could get the right angle for best results. In times past, he would have called the medical photographer to make the picture and wait for it to be printed out. But now, Ron used his phone with high-resolution camera and had a portable photograph, front and each side, in less than five minutes. As he and the diener worked on getting the photograph, Gene stayed near the entrance and thumbed through his emails on his phone.

When Ron was satisfied with his photos, he thanked the diener for his help and walked over to Gene.

'What do you think, partner?" he asked.

Gene took a quick look, "She still looks dead. Can't we get the Registrar to give us a photo from her admission application?"

"Maybe. If we knew who she was." Ron turned back to where Darringer was standing and said, "Thanks, Doc. I hope we didn't hold you up."

Darringer was staring at her phone. She said, "No worries. I just got a call about another DB, so I won't get to this one till tomorrow morning. Come join me for the First Case."

"If we can." And the detectives let them selves out as Darringer pulled off the gown covering her clothes.

Gene didn't speak until they were in the car. Staring off out the side window, he commenting as if he were discussing the weather, "I wish you hadn't promised her we would come back for the post."

Ron knew of the hesitation his partner had to attending autopsies. But he felt strongly that the mental Rembrandt of the damage one person had done to another was a powerful dynamic that kept homicide detectives pushing for answers until the perp was caught. He said, "You know I think this is an important part of 'discovery' in a murder investigation, don't you?"

"Sure, I do. But Darringer gets on my nerves. And spending any time in that room is a major downer."

"You mean the 'laboratory'?"

"Yep. Laboratory, my ass. Laboratories are on the fifth floor with big windows, lots of light and got several tables holding scientific equipment and stuff. Her 'laboratory' is a morgue, gray floor, gray walls, that operating table in the middle of the room with that overhanging light reminds me of Dr. Frankenstein's laboratory."

Ron nodded sagely, waiting for Gene's next move, which was not long in coming.

"I gotta have something to eat. Settle my stomach, you know."

Ron agreed and Gene insisted that they once again stop by the coffee shop on their way to campus. This time they ended up sitting at a back table while Gene ate a jelly-filled doughnut.

"What have you got there, partner?" Ron asked.

"Strawberry."

I thought we only got those here around Easter."

"Mardi Gras."

"Oh, yeah. Right. Until I got here I always thought Mardi Gras was a New Orleans thing."

"It is."

"You know, I could get to like this. You and doughnuts," Ron said sipping his coffee.

"Whyszat?" Gene mumbled around a large bite that threatened to put most of the jelly fill on the table.

"Because you don't talk as much."

"I resemble that remark," Gene fired back, catching the errant jelly.

"I knew a guy in the service from North Dakota," Ron went on. "He called those jelly-filled things a 'Bismarck'. I never got an explanation. Maybe he thought they were all made in the state capital."

"Alright. I'm finished. Where're we going first?" Gene wiped his mouth and took a swig of his coffee.

Ron looked thoughtful for a minute, and then said, "As we discussed, our best shot at finding out whether this girl was a student or not is through the registrar's office."

"OK. What if she's not a student?"

"I don't know. Let's start with the most likely. She's on campus, she's probably a student. And once we have a name we can really get started. Friends, teachers, family, and like that."

"I'm ready," Gene said taking a swallow of his coffee.

"And I promise we will take time for lunch and you can see Sandra."

"Good of you. I'm seeing her almost every night now. But more is better."

They took Linn northward and cut under 127 after Bank Street and took the little jig in the street on McMicken Avenue to get to Ravine. As they headed north and passed Fairview Park, Gene asked, "Is this spring, yet? I think I'm seeing some color out there in the Park."

'Yeah. Probably crocus. I've got some in my yard that just appeared yesterday."

"Spring, then."

"Look off to the right down town. We can almost see where those demonstrators were last night."

"I'm glad nobody got killed. I really wouldn't want to try to untangle anything from that mess."

"We are alike in that sentiment, partner."

At McMillan, Looney turned right and followed the major avenue to the corner at the STEM High School. He made the left onto Clifton and the right onto the campus on McMicken Circle. They found a parking place right near the Pavilion.

As they started across the street, Looney pointed to the grass growing in the sidewalk cracks. "Another sign that spring is here, Gene. In the next month we'll have to start mowing our sidewalks."

The Pavilion housing most of the administrative office of the University sat back from the Circle and they approached on a wide mosaic tile walkway. At the Registrar's office Ron asked to speak with Registrar himself and was met by a short, thin man with abundant brown hair and horn-rimmed glasses wearing a dark brown suit and a maroon vest.

"Mr. Rigby?" Ron asked.

"Dr. Rigby. Can I help you?""

"Yes, of course. Dr. Rigby. I'm Detective Ron Looney, this is my partner, Gene Novalchek. We'd like your help?"

"Is this about the young woman you found this morning?"

"Yes. We'd like to know if she is a student."

"Of course. And I am the one to answer that question."

"Excellent," said Ron, with some encouragement that this might not be as difficult as feared.

"Of course," said Rigby. "What is her name?"

The detectives looked at each other, caught by the question. "We don't know," Gene said, looking surprised. "We were coming here to get that kind of information."

"And how did you imagine I would be able to know that and help you?"

"You're the Registrar, right?" Ron asked and as Rigby nodded, he went on, "And we thought you, or someone in the office could recognize her from this picture." He took out the morgue picture and showed it to Rigby.

The man moved back from the offered picture and said, "I rarely encounter the students. Perhaps one of my staff can help you."

"That would be great," Gene said.

They were introduced to the staff in the office that regularly interacted with the students but found no one who recognized the picture.

"Do you have pictures of all students?" Ron inquired.

After a short pause of the staff looking about and at each other one replied, "Not all."

"Why not?"

"Well, the Admissions Office would have a picture on every application but we just deal with the registration and payment for course work. We usually do all that electronically. I mean we don't really even see most of the students here."

Ron pondered for a moment then said, "If I wanted to find pictures of all the students to compare with this picture, where would I go?"

"Admissions," several people said at once, nodding vigorously.

"Or the library," said a quiet voice in the back.

"What was that?" asked Gene, pointing toward the diminutive young woman in the plain dress at the rear of the room..

"I said, you could try the library," she said, with a voice that trailed off uncertainly.

"Why the library?" asked Ron.

"If she checked out any books or put any on reserve for study, the librarians would have seen her," came the sensible answer, more sure of itself.

"That's a good idea, thanks," Ron said and started for the door. Gene was already heading that way and grabbed the door handle and pulled it open.

"Or you could look her up in the yearbooks."

Ron slowed as he approached the door, consciously refrained from slapping his forehead and said, "Or I could look in the yearbooks."

CHAPTER 5

T he Langsam Library was some distance away and Looney moved his car to the parking deck on Woodside. They entered across from the parking structure and found themselves on the wrong side of the building. With help from students they were able to find their way into the main entry area where large windows looked out onto the piazza in front of the building.

"Not much like the two-story red brick building in Squashton," Looney said. Gene let the comment go and pointed to a large desk with friendly-appearing young women behind them. The librarians were uniformly helpful but not to the extent of actually identifying the dead girl. At least two of the librarians were confident she was a student, remembering her at some point using the library services. However, no one knew her name. Encouraged by this information the detectives asked for the two most recent yearbooks and sat down to carefully page through them.

At Ron's suggestion they each started at different 'ends' of the pictorial books, He started with the senior class and moved backward through the pages while Gene started with the most recent incoming freshman class and worked upward. Almost an hour passed with minimal comments between the two. They sat across a table from each other, slowly turning the pages of the yearbooks and scanning photographs and comparing them to their morgue picture. As they started Ron reminded Gene not to pay too much attention to the hair color in the morgue photograph since the girl might have changed the color since her picture was taken. After a few minutes of quiet page turning, Gene mentioned that one girl he saw looked a great deal like one of his nieces; a little later Ron showed him a picture of someone that looked like a television or movie star but he could not remember the name. Gene agreed and they went back to their respective silences.

Ron thought if you really did ignore the hairdo and the hair color, a great many of these pictures began to seem as if they were of the same person. All the young women had open eyes, a smile and an upturned chin. Except for cheekbone differences and occasionally skin tone, the faces were eerily similar. There were no worry lines, no wrinkles and no scars. These were faces that had come to the photographer without much cost of living.

"Bingo," said Gene said enthusiastically after a prolonged period of quiet. "I got her."

"Let's see," Ron said.

Gene turned the book around and moved it across the table toward his partner. Ron held up his copy of the morgue photo and smiled at his partner. "I give you Bingo."

"Name is Margaret Kuykendahl. She is a sophomore, interested in communication, theatre and art."

"Address?"

"There is not an address in the Yearbook. We 'll have to look elsewhere."

"Then we are going back to the registrar's Office."

"And I am so looking forward to that."

*　*　*

Dr. Rigby was, as he had predicted, quite helpful once he was supplied with a name. He directed his personnel to obtain appropriate information and soon the detectives were in possession of Margaret's local address in a dormitory, her parents names and address in a small town near Cleveland as well as telephone numbers for both Margaret's cell phone and her parents' home. They thanked the staff and Dr. Rigby for their help and got information about how to locate the dormitory where Margaret had lived.

As per protocol, as soon as they left the Registrar's office Ron called the Medical Examiner.

"Darringer," she answered.

"Doc, it's Walker. We got the girl's name and address. You up for calling it in?"

"Yes, I'll call the local authorities and they will go to the house to talk with the family. They will give my number for further information. Do you want me to refer them to you?"

"Not right now. You can tell them that I will be calling them for a short interview soon." He recited the information they had just received from the Registrar's office.

"And if they don't call me?" Darringer asked after she got the information.

"Well, give the local guys my name and number and they can pass it on. I'll likely call later today to talk to the parents."

"I'll let them know. Was she a student?"

"Yeah. Sophomore. By the way, when are you gonna do the post?"

"It's still up for first thing in the morning."

"Gene will love that. Right after breakfast."

"That's why I stock barf bags in the lab."

"See you in the morning, then."

CHAPTER 6

"This is her dorm. Third floor," Ron said as they turned from the main sidewalk.

"Does anybody ever live on the first floor?"

"I remember one case back in '15 when we only had to walk one flight."

"But that was because the crime scene was on the second floor."

"Yeah, you're right. That's the funny thing about floors. Some places it's a First Floor and across the street it's the Ground Floor and First is up one flight."

"I just know that both of my kids dorm rooms in college were on the third floor. Every year."

They took their time on the stairs so as not to create a feeling of rush or anxiety. Several students passed going down and paid little attention to them. Apparently grown men in suits were not uncommon in the women's dormitory. Ron was the father of a recent college graduate who lived in the women's dormitory and he had wondered about this lax attitude back then.

They located Margaret's room and knocked on the door.

"Yes?" from a female voice inside the room.

"Ms. Spradley?" said Ron. The door opened and they were faced with a smallish girl, who appeared to be in her late teens, about five foot five inches in jeans and a sweater and whose hair was exceptionally unkempt. She was holding a towel.

"No one calls me 'Ms Spradley'. Who are you?" she asked and resumed toweling her hair.

"I'm Detective Ron Looney and this is my partner, Gene Novalchek," Ron answered as they help out their identification and badges for inspection.

"We'd like to talk to you about Margaret."

"Peggy? She's not here. I really don't know where she is. What's this all about? And you can call me Helen."

"May we come in?"

"Uh, yeah, I guess," she said, backing into the room and increasing the speed of drying her hair with the towel.

The dorm room was small and very tidy. Two beds, placed on opposite sides of the room with two desks, and an easy chair that occupied most of the walk space in front of a large closet.

Helen Spradley indicated the easy chair and one of the desk chairs and then sat down on the foot of her bed. "What's this about?" she asked again.

"When was the last time you saw Ms. Kuykendahl?" Ron asked.

After a brief pause in the toweling, Helen put the towel in her lap and fixed Ron with a questioning look. "Where is she?"

Gene started to ask the question a second time but Ron interrupted him, "She's dead, Ms Spradley... uh, Helen."

"Oh, Migod. No. Are you sure it's Peggy?"

"Is this Peggy?" he asked, showing her the morgue photo.

She paled and her small frame slumped into the bed. She dropped the towel and showed no interest in it.

"What . .I mean . . What happened?" she wanted to know. Her eyes watered up and she sniffed back some tears and bobbed her head.

"She was found this morning on campus."

"What do you mean, like 'found'?" Helen asked with a slight tremor in her voice, as if she already knew Ron's meaning.

After a slight pause, Ron continued, "She was killed by someone during the night and that person left her on campus like she was sleeping outdoors."

"That's why she didn't come home."

"You didn't see her last night?"

"No. Oh Migod. This is terrible. Who's going to tell her parents?"

"The authorities are taking care of that. Do you know her parents?"

"Not really. I mean we met when she moved in back in September. What happened to her?"

"We really don't know much right now. We are just starting to look into things."

"Oh Migod. This is terrible."

"When did you last see her?"

"Umm, yesterday morning, I guess."

"About what time?"

"Right after class, I guess. Maybe 11:30."

"And what was she doing?"

"She said she was going to take a nap. I had two classes in the afternoon and I left her here."

"Was that usual for her. To nap in the morning?"

"Well, sometimes. If she had a date that night, yeah."

"Did she have a date last night?"

"I don't know. I mean, she didn't say so. But she usually stayed out late if she did."

"How late?"

"Like, you know, after midnight always, sometimes later."

"Was she dating anyone in particular?"

"Yeah, I think so. I don't know who. Some guy."

"Why don't you know? Didn't she ever talk about him"

"Not really, I mean she was like, you know, really mum on him."

"How long had she been seeing him?"

"Not long, I think. Maybe just like a couple of weeks."

"Name?"

Helen shook her head. Further questioning gained very little about this mystery person. Margaret's dates with him were always late at night and her habit of napping beforehand was a recent change in her behavior. The detectives pressed for any information such as a distant sighting, mention of his habits, facial hair, anything. Helen was increasingly saddened and depressed about the death and became less and less helpful.

Finally, Ron said, "We appreciate your time, Ms Spradley. If you think of anything else, please give me a call," as he handed her his card. She accepted the card absent-mindedly and did not look up as Ron and Gene excused themselves and left the room and the dormitory.

CHAPTER 7

As time stretched toward suppertime, Ron and Gene walked the third floor hall and interviewed other young women living there. No one admitted to being particularly close to Margaret although they all knew her. Apparently Margaret had joined the theatre group on campus and did not pledge a sorority, as had virtually every other girl on the hall. Consequently, Margaret was not involved in the usual and many Greek activities in the life of the campus. She was known as quiet, studious but most of the women interviewed referred to her as 'Helen's roommate'.

Two of the young women mentioned that Margaret had been seen talking to the Resident Advisor or RA on the floor recently and the detectives decided to interview her last. Her room was in the area where the center hall was bisected by the stairway. The detectives took up their waiting in the hall for the advisor to return to the floor and to her room.

"Did you ever live like this?" Ron asked Gene indicating the hallway to his right by pointing his chin.

"You mean in a college dorm?"

"Yeah. Did you?"

"Yes, my first year in college. Everyone had to live in a dorm. University rules; probably to weed out the ones having trouble adjusting. That's what I thought. Found out later it was a totally financial reason. Administration had built dorms and they needed the income from student renters to stay solvent. Got permission to live off campus after that."

"What's it like?"

"Uh, bunch of guys in small quarters. Three to a room, shared toilet and shower for the hall. High androgen level, so fair amount of pushing and towel snapping and body odor." He studied Ron a bit and then asked, "Why? Didn't you have something like that in the service?"

"Well, in a way. There certainly were a bunch of guys living in a small area with all the testosterone and odor but we were not in that space for much of the day. We were out training, running five miles in full pack or drilling. And, there was a universal 'lights out' and a loud voice at 0530 reminding us that our rest period was over. So, no, not exactly."

"What's this R.A.'s name again?"

"Roxanne Sevier," Ron said consulting his notepad.

"Wonder if she's a 'Roxie'?"

"I wonder if she's Ms Sevier."

"Here she comes. You ask her," Gene said standing up and indicating the dark-haired young woman coming up the stairs.."

"Roxie Sevier?"

"Yes. Can I help you?"

"We'd like to talk with you about Margaret Kuykendahl. I'm Detective Ron Looney. This is my partner, Gene Novalchek."

"What about Margaret?"

"Could we step inside your room, please?" Ron asked. After a brief pause, Roxie assented and opened her door using her key. It was as spare as others but contained only a single bed. Roxie indicated the detectives could sit in the chairs at the study desk. She then took a seat on the foot of the bed, turned to Ron, and raised her eyebrows.

Ron recognized the implicit question and asked, "Are you aware that she was killed early this morning?"

"Oh, no!"

"I'm afraid so. Could we ask you a few questions?" "This is terrible,"What happened?"

"It appears that she was killed on campus early this morning possibly by someone she knew."

"Do her parents know? She was so sweet. This is terrible!"

"How well did you know her?

"Not much at all until recently."

"What was different recently?"

"She was asking me about becoming an RA next year and she wanted to know about the responsibilities and all that. So we met a couple of times here in my room and once, I think, no may be twice, in the cafeteria. Do you know who did this?"

"We are interested in talking with a fellow she was reportedly dating. Do you know anything about that?"

"No, I don't. We didn't talk about her social life. I mean we just talked about living on the Dorm hall and looking out for the girls. She wanted to do that next year, money I guess."

"Money?"

"Sure. We get free room and board and a small stipend. I think that was a big reason for her interest. What are we to do about this?"

"Her family is being notified. My partner and I have talked to her roommate …"

"Helen."

"Yes, Helen."

"We will continue to investigate and we would like you to let us know if you remember anything in the future," Ron said as he handed her his card.

"And I'm going to have a job counseling with all her friends on the hall," Roxanne said.

"Maybe that won't take as long as you think," Gene said as they left.

CHAPTER 8

The concept of a laboratory may bring certain mental images to mind and usually widely different mental Rembrandts for different people. Some see a brightly lit room full of long tables topped by various machines like incubators, or large centrifuges and racks of test tubes filled with differently colored liquids. Others may conjure up visions of dusty tall cases with glass doors and several tables covered by bizarre glassware and multiple Bunsen burners in a dark cellar. Or anything in between.

Dr. Darringer's 'laboratory' looked almost exactly like every other city morgue. Gray painted concrete flooring slanted into a large, centrally placed drain, walls of puke colored ceramic tile on the bottom half, Industrial gray paint on the top. One wall held a series of refrigerated mortuary cabinets, three high and eight in length. Between the drain and the wall on each side was a metal non-vented autopsy table with an over-hanging operating room light and affixed with a hanging microphone operated by a foot pedal. This room was and forever will be a morgue.

But Dr. Darringer's approach to her work in the morgue had always been one of scientific examination; thus, this room was her area for conducting scientific inquiry, asking hard questions and seeking best answers. In short, as far as she was concerned, she worked in a laboratory. And she told everyone that.

The room was in the basement of the County Medical Examiner's building and was predominantly lit by artificial light. But there were small windows atop the walls, at ground level outside. Through these small apertures one could discern whether it was day or night, barely, but not much else.

Shortly after eight in the morning, Ron and Gene made their cautious way into the 'laboratory' to watch the autopsy on Margaret Kuykendahl. The M.E. had already repeated her external examination of the body and was preparing to make the 'Y' incision when they arrived. Kathryn Darringer looked more like someone's grandmother than the Cincinnati City Medical Examiner. She was five foot eight inches and solidly built with a broad face and expressive blue eyes. Her hair was light brown and streaked with gray but always neat and kept out of her face. Her wide mouth was commonly slanted in a wry grin as if she had just discovered something inappropriately humorous. When she put on her apron for a post-mortem and her wire-framed glasses, she mostly resembled a grandmother busily working in her kitchen. The image of a friendly, cookie-cooking grandmother changed, however, when she donned the surgical cap and face shield. Darringer nodded to indicate a greeting to the detectives but did not take her foot off the recording pedal.

"Margaret Kuykendahl, age 21, 118 pounds, five foot 5 inches is a white female appearing in good nutritional health and with no external body marks, scars or tattoos," she recorded.

"Entering the chest after the usual 'Y' incision, there is no excess fluid or macroscopic injury or disease affecting her lungs or her heart," she went on. Dr. Darringer did not pause in her recitation of findings - all of which were normal - until she began the examination of the lower abdomen.

At that point Ron moved closer to the table and interrupted, "Any evidence of sexual activity?"

"That depends on your definition and what you are looking for, detective."

"What I meant to ask . . ."

"Was whether she had recent sexual intercourse," the doctor said flatly.

"Yes."

"No. She did not. I did a rape kit yesterday when we brought her in. There was no evidence of recent sexual activity."

"But…?"

"But she was not a virgin."

Ron stepped back and Darringer continued with her gross anatomical examination. When she was finished and had turned to the specimen table to begin examining various organs more carefully, Looney asked,

"How about a couple of things to fill in some gaps?"

"And that would be?"

"Time of death to start with."

"Probably between 12:30 and 1:30 yesterday morning. "What was that stuff in her stomach?"

"Can't be completely sure right now but there was coffee in the mix."

"Anything else you can tell us about the cause of death?"

"See the X-Rays on the box over there?"

"Yep."

"I know you know something about this, Detective Looney. What do you see?"

Ron walked over the to view box with Gene right behind him. The radiographs were obviously taken to show the head and neck from one side. Ron took his time and studied the films briefly before answering, "This is a shot of her neck from the side and the vertebrae in her neck are broken."

"Excellent. If she had, say, accidentally fallen and struck her head by falling forward or backward with enough force to snap her neck, the vertebrae would have been compressed on either the anterior or posterior surface. And that is not what we see." She paused before continuing, "What else do you see Detective Looney?"

"The bone parts look like they were moved twisted and sideways."

"Absolutely right." She waited and when he did not go on, she asked, "And what kind of injury causes that?"

"I think you are steering me toward saying this was a 'neck snap'. Right, doc?" He turned abruptly to face the doctor.

"That is exactly what I think it is," she said.

"Hold on guys," Gene said, breaking in. "What're we talking about here with this 'neck snap' idea?"

Dr. Darringer answered, "The force that killed her was a twisting force that rotated her head and lifted her chin, snapping her neck vertebrae and slicing the spinal cord."

"Geez," he said. "What does it take to do that?"

"Strength," she answered, simply.

"Training." Ron added.

"What kind of training? Military? Or are we looking for an MMA fighter?" Gene asked.

"Military probably," Ron said quietly. "Not general training, though. This is Special Ops training. Certainly not MMA. This move kills and that would be bad for television ratings."

CHAPTER 9

They sat in the car and Gene attempted to put a little structure to their findings. "First," he said, "looks like we have a Means with this recognition of the 'neck snap' thing. And there's clear Opportunity with the little green area at one in the morning on a quiet campus." He looked at Ron for some feedback and saw a deliberate nod. "Now all we have to do is find the Motive."

Ron nodded again and commented, "Well, there's always the bothersome little question of 'Who' had that Opportunity."

"Yeah," Gene agreed, "probably comes down to the same two we always start off with: someone she knew or a stranger."

"But even the 'someone she knew' comes in different flavors," Ron noted scratching his chin.

Gene nodded, "You mean someone she knew and had been out with versus someone she just knew in passing."

"And if it was someone she knew, why kill her?"

"Maybe they had a fight?"

"Pretty big disagreement to have someone end up dead. And the scene didn't support a fight - at least not a physical one."

"The evidence supports that they knew each other and they were familiar enough for her to let this person get behind her."

"Right. Maybe it was someone she knew from elsewhere who just happened to be hanging around the park."

"At midnight? That doesn't sound happenstance."

"Maybe not for someone from off campus. But what about someone else who is also 'just getting back'?"

"Or someone from that protest downtown coming back to the campus and sees a chance to create more violence and tension?"

"You think that's likely?"

"Did you look at the protesters? They're not rabble-rousers and druggies. They are all dressed in designer jeans and Ts and they're mostly college-age. I bet there's a lot of the college kids getting involved in the 'protest fun'.

"I can believe it but that's crazy. There was no fun in the Watts riots or when Martin Luther King, Jr. got shot. Or in Minneapolis."

"You know that and I know that but these kids fantasize about the 60's like those were the good old days. Protests and riots seem romantic at this distance."

With that puzzling thought in mind both men sat back in their seat and thought for minute.

After a bit of silence, Gene asked, "How's it with your Dad?' Ron was quiet and initially appeared as if he had not heard the question. Then, staring straight ahead he said quietly, "About the same, No real improvement."

"Sorry, man. You going back down anytime soon?"

"Maybe. If'n we get time and don't have a case hanging over us." Ron sat staring out the windscreen and Gene decided he had already said too much and joined in the silence.

Ron thought back to that early morning call weeks before from his brother, Ken. "Dad's had a stroke. We've got him at the hospital in Pine Bluff." Straightforward, simple declarative sentences, right to the heart of the matter; Ken was very much like their father.

Ron had gotten the rest of the story, slowly from Ken and from his mother. Hal Looney, Ron's dad, had awakened early that morning with paralysis of the left side of his face and left arm. He woke his wife and she and Ken determined he should go to the hospital. They made the trip before the sun arose in south Arkansas. Doctors at the Regional Medical Center diagnosed the stroke everyone had suspected but had no therapy for Hal because of the timing of the onset during sleep.

Hal had been admitted and was being monitored while the physicians tried to determine if he was at risk of additional strokes from heart problems or other conditions. Ron had made the necessary arrangements and flew out of Cincinnati a couple of hours later. He had rented a car in Memphis and drove directly to the Jefferson Regional Medical Center in Pine Bluff.

Ron had not been back home for almost five years at that point and he was struck by how much older his brother and mother looked when he met them in the lobby of the Medical Center. His mother looked as if she had visibly shrunk in height by several inches and his brother was considerably broader across the chest than Ron remembered. Those memories came back to him as he sat in the car, wondering about his father's condition anew since Gene had raised the question.

Back then, Ron had stayed in Arkansas for three days. He talked with the doctors and the physical therapists about prognosis but the important talk was with his father. Ron had stayed at the hospital that first night and he and Hal had talked about many things: how the kids were doing, whether he was still working with the CPD, the spring planting, the worry about enough rain, and finally, what Hal thought he was going to do with the farm.

Hal had already relied on Ken to do most of the work and many of the crop and storage decisions in the past two years, so he felt comfortable with that arrangement. The understanding seemed right to Ron, as well. He had no personal interest in the farm or the land and he believed Ken would handle things correctly. Ron had an opportunity to talk with Ken about that plan after Hal's discharge and during the trip back to Squashton. The brothers had not really been close growing up since they were seven years apart and Ron's decision to join the Air Force right out of high school precluded any shared experiences on the farm.

Ron knew that Ken, the oldest, was really almost a clone of their father. They had the same face and rolling walk. They argued the same points in any discussion and almost always came to identical decisions. Ron knew the farm would be safe in Ken's hands. He lived there on the homestead with his wife and three boys so there were plenty of hands to help out.

Ron had enjoyed two days of his mother's cooking and carefully refrained from any comparison between that and what Meg prepared. When he finally left it was only after promising to make trips home more often, although he doubted that he would actually do so for several years. His drive back to Memphis was uneventful and gave him time to evaluate the changes he experienced at the farm. The hog pen seemed much smaller than he remembered when one of his regular chores was to heave a bucket of slop over the fence and into the pen. The pen also was much closer to the house now, he thought, as he remembered the long journey from house to pen carrying the slop bucket.

Even though he had spent 18 years in that town and on that farm, Ron was caught unawares by the way that time seemed to slow down in Squashton and at the farm. These people were rooted to the soil and the cycles of day to night, spring to summer, and rain to sunshine. Their recognition of the certainty of those cycles removed most of their anxiety about 'tomorrow' or even 'next year' in a way that Ron thought city people couldn't understand or mimic. He missed that feeling of certainty but he also knew that he had become not only a 'city boy' while he had been absent from the farm, he was also a cop. And no cop does a good job being relaxed and 'certain' of the future.

Even as Ron realized the magnitude of the change in his life between Squashton, Arkansas and Cincinnati, Ohio, he also realized how much he appreciated what he had in Cincinnati. That remembrance caused him to press the accelerator and to exceed the speed limit on I-40 getting to Memphis to catch a plane so he could return 'home'.

Ron suddenly realized he had not spoken to Gene for several minutes during this reverie. He turned toward his partner and said, "Actually, Dad's doing well and adjusting to his arm paralysis. He still gets up before dawn and walks with Ken around the farmyard. And they're making money so 'no worries'."

Gene nodded, realizing that his partner had been away in his thoughts and had only just then come back to work. Carefully, not wanting to insult, he took a deep breath, shifted in his seat and stared out the front window as he asked, "So, if you had to bet would you put your money on someone she knew or a stranger?"

After a short pause Ron answered, " Someone she knew. The scene was too serene for a stranger. Let's push that idea until it collapses."

CHAPTER 10

They paused around lunchtime. They had retraced their steps back to the registrar's office and obtained a copy of Margaret's class schedule and began tracking down relevant teachers. To their good fortune the first one they sought was not actively teaching and had just finished a student conference. She was the professor for the English Literature course and remembered Margaret well. According to the professor Margaret had been an above average student, interested in the material and timely in handing in work assignments. However, the professor did not regard Margaret as among the best students in the class; her written assignments were complete but without depth or particular insight, always on time and with no evidence of having any outside 'influence', as she mentioned twice.

When pressed about the reference to 'outside influence' the professor explained she was referring to evident plagiarism such as copying commentaries from widely available Internet sources or having someone else to write her work for her. She explained that one of her first activities for students in the class was to have them write a short history of their life and experiences on the first day of class. She had them write this by hand and turn it in before leaving the classroom; the assignment was to provide enough breadth and length that would fill two pages of paper. The professor used this information to better understand her charges particularly in interpreting their analyses of literature. But thereafter she had a handwriting sample for each student as well as a fair sample of their writing including word usage, sentence structure, phrasing and even punctuation. The clever professor then regularly used that standard to compare each student's work assignments to their own known work to determine whether they were providing their own thoughts or not.

The professor admitted that she usually caught at least one student using 'outside influence' every semester but had assured the detectives that Margaret did not seem to be one. She had no idea about her outside of class activities or even whether she was friendly with any others in the class.

When they caught up with the second instructor at eleven o'clock, she had just finished a class period and was free until after lunch. The three of them sat in her crowded office for the interview. The small office was cluttered with stacks of books on top of filing cabinets and even on the floor. There was only a single chair, antique wooden and straight-backed, in addition to the instructor's chair behind her desk. The desktop was also cluttered with papers and folders and an occasional book. The instructor was a graduate student teaching the class as part of a degree requirement in marketing.

She knew Margaret only as one of many in the class and had noted no specific interest between Margaret and others in the class. In fact, the instructor was not certain where Margaret normally sat in the classroom.

Ron wanted to grab something to eat in the school cafeteria but Gene wanted them to go back and visit Sandra and after a short argument about the time away from the job they returned to Sandra's place of work. Seated across from each other in a booth along the sidewall, Gene's view of Sandra working tables was limited to the front half of the café.

"I'm just saying, Ron, if we had come earlier like I said, we could've been in that booth up front."

"I'm just as sure that you are right about that. But then we would have spent twice as long to get lunch while you stare at Sandra."

"I am not staring. I'm watching her. She considers my attention as 'appreciation'."

"They called it ogling when I was a kid. Or maybe it was gawking."

"Whatever."

"So, we are nowhere on these interviews."

"This Margaret really was a quiet one. No obvious friends. No one she hung around with."

"No favorite café for lunch. Really hinders our style." Ron made this crack as Sandra came to the table for their order. She smiled perfunctorily at him and then really beamed at Gene. "The usual, honey?"

"Sure, Sandy. All the way."

"And I'll have that, too," Ron interjected. Sandy nodded without turning and left the table.

"So, it's 'honey' now is it?" Ron asked with faux seriousness.

"All right, calm down. Yes, it's honey. And I like it, so leave it be." Gene did not sound all that perturbed and the eyebrows stayed apart so Ron knew his partner was not truly offended. "Good for you," he whispered. "But, by the way, what am I getting as 'the usual'?"

"Patty melt with potato chips and iced tea."

"OK, then. Patty melt it is. Still, we gotta find some kind of lead here or Thor is going to replace us on this case."

"I don't think he's got anyone that can do better. We just need to keep going forward. But I'm beginning to think there isn't much for us on the campus. I mean, look at it. We talked to her roommate and her Resident Advisor. We talked to all those other girls on the hall. We've heard from her teachers that she's quiet and unimaginative and not a cheater."

"And apparently she had no friends on campus but started dating an unknown a few weeks back."

"It's like tracking a ghost in a snowstorm."

"It is starting to look that way. But there's still one place we haven't checked," Ron said leaning back in the booth. "We still need to talk to her history professor."

CHAPTER 11

Sandy brought their food and paid slightly more attention to Ron as he examined his plate.

"I can get you more potato chips if you'd like," she said looking right at him.

H smiled at her and replied, "Thanks, Sandy. I believe these will be sufficient." She smiled back at him for knowing her name and went back to the kitchen.

Ron looked at Gene who was already into his patty melt. "That girl's smile light up a room, Gene."

"Hmm."

After lunch Ron followed the now familiar practice; he put down his money and left to go bring the car around to the front of the café to pick up Gene. This left Gene to talk to Sandra for a few minutes. He rarely left Ron sitting in the car outside for long. And he always seemed in the best of moods when he did get in the car.

On the way back toward campus Gene commented, "Looks like we have only the one other professor to talk with. Dr. Rathmore. Sounds like someone out of a Sherlock Holmes story."

"He teaches Western Civilization from the Four Princes to the Reformation."

"Yeah, I read the same briefer you did. Who were these four princes, anyway?"

"I looked them up. The group includes Henry VIII of England, Francis I of France, Charles V of the Holy Roman Empire and Suleiman I, of the Ottoman Empire."

"Princes? Those guys were kings!"

'And referred to as 'princes' by historians."

"Who's that last guy?"

"Suleiman, Sultan of the Ottoman Empire."

"What's with him and the other three?"

"That why you should study history, bud. And that's why there's a whole course on these guys in college."

"I've heard of the first guys."

"Did you know they were all contemporaries?"

"No, I did not. That's actually kinda interesting"

"As was Suleiman. And Suleiman was trying to invade Europe from Turkey during that time."

"So these three other guys and the sultan were all tangled up?"

"Oh yeah."

"How'd you know about that?"

"Read a book. Meg gave me this book for Christmas a year ago. Fun to see history that isn't all those dull dates and stuff. Got some meat on the bones."

As Ron pulled into a parking slot, Gene offered, "Let's just hope Dr. History can shed some light on Margaret."

Dr. Barry Rathmore was also in his office and available for interview. Rathmore appeared to be the quintessential college professor. Tall and thin, he wore a blue oxford cloth shirt with a striped bow tie, dark trousers and an aged tweed jacket with leather patches on both elbows. Ron surmised that the man probably drove a Volkswagen Squareback and smoked a pipe, as well. Rathmore invited the detectives in and indicated they could sit in the two chairs in front of his desk. He was appropriately surprised at the information concerning Margaret's death and asked what he could do to help. Ron was equally surprised to see no evidence of an ashtray or pipes on the man's desk.

The professor's memory of Margaret Kuykendahl was somewhat better-and different-from the previous interviews. He remembered that Margaret and another student, Susan Harrington, had a 'dust-up' as he called it in class a few weeks before. His academic assignments involved students posting opinions on a shared website along with answers about questions he would pose from assigned reading or lecture material. Their post, on the official class distance learning site was required by a certain time and before they posted their own response, students could not see what others wrote. After their initial entry, students were expected to read what others had written and engage in further discussion. The 'dust-up' occurred over a difference of opinion about what Susan thought Margaret had implied about her. She responded with vigor and some vitriol online and brought that displeasure to the next class.

Rathmore remembered that the comment Margaret had made was clumsily written but was in fact a criticism of the thought process of one of the princes, not of Susan's comment about the prince. He said the classroom discussion was actually led by other students who correctly interpreted Margaret's comment and they helped calm Susan down. And Margaret had publicly apologized for bad writing and hurt feelings. Everyone seemed calmer after that and the rest of the class time was without disruption. Rathmore said Margaret and Susan were talking calmly to each other after the class.

Ron and Gene each realized that they had exhausted their leads on campus. Seamlessly, each of them began to think about next steps and how to begin to narrow down a field containing the ghost in the snowstorm. Ron thanked Dr. Rathmore for his time, and he and Gene stood, and walked to the door. Turning at the last moment, Ron said,

"If you should think of anything else, give me a call." He stepped back toward the professor's desk and handed him one of his cards. The professor looked at the card thoughtfully and, as Ron turned back to the door, he asked, "Have you talked with her social group in the theatre?"

CHAPTER 12

After they got directions to the campus theatre, they got caught in a short rain shower and ran into a classroom building to wait for the skies to clear. As they stood in the archway entrance a couple of students ran past them into the building, holding coats over their heads and ignoring the detectives.

"I really don't like the rain," Gene offered.

"City kid, weren't you?" Ron asked.

"Well, yeah. Why?"

"City kids think the rain just makes a day dreary. It gets in the way of your plans, which never include rain. It's entirely different with kids that grew up like me. Farm kids know that's what makes the crops grow and puts food on the table. Plus it usually means no outside chores."

"Well, yeah, I know that."

"But that knowledge is not something ingrained in your bone marrow, so you see the rain as an impediment to your day. It slows you down. You get depressed thinking about it."

"Impediment? Really? I think I don't like the rain on a workday because it will ruin my suit if I get it wet. That's all."

"Impediment. But I think it's even deeper than lack of knowledge, my friend. Or actually, now that I think about it, a lot more shallow."

"Pooh. I thought you hated the rain. Don't you tell that story about having to walk to school in the rain?"

"That's snow. I had to walk five miles to school in the snow. That's frozen rain. Uphill it was, too. Both ways."

"Farmers," Gene said dismissively.

"You betcha, city slicker."

When the rain slacked up and then ceased, they made for the Theatre and arrived before the rain started up again. As they entered the front door they heard the sound of a table saw to their right but there was no one is sight. They found themselves in a wide hallway with large bulletin boards on each side and doors to side rooms far down the hall.

They opened some double doors on the right that led into a large classroom with folding chairs placed haphazardly around the perimeter. Again, no one was evident but the sound of the saw was louder and seemed to come from the rear of the classroom. They crossed the room and found a doorway in the rear.

Ron opened the door in the back wall and the saw sound became louder. They went down a short hallway to another large room behind open double doors that held the running table saw. A couple of young men were also in the room; one was working to cut several pieces of 2x4s to identical lengths and the other was stacking them on a cart. They were intent on their construction activity and were unaware that anyone had entered the room.

"Hey guys," Ron called out, getting their immediate attention. The saw was silenced.

"We're detectives and we'd like to ask you a few questions, OK?"

Solemn nods and shrugs all about and Ron got right underway with his questions as Gene watched everyone's reactions. "Do any of you know Margaret Kuykendahl?"

The young man who had been working the saw just stared at Ron but the other one said, "Peggy? Yeah, I know her. She's not here. We're set production. She's Live E."

"What's Live E?" Gene asked, truly puzzled.

"Live Entertainment. Actor. The talent."

"How well do you know her?" Ron persisted.

"I know who she is, that's all."

"Friends?"

"No, she runs with the rest of the talent."

"Meaning what, exactly?"

"I mean after rehearsal, she goes out with the other actors. For coffee and like that."

"Who does she usually go out with?"

"I dunno. Maybe Audrey. They usually rehearse together."

"Where would we find Audrey?"

"Dorm, I guess."

Since the set production guys were unaware of what dorm this Audrey lived in, Ron called the Registrar, Dr. Rigby to obtain that information. He also helped with the location of that dormitory.

The rain had ceased completely and they walked quickly back to Ron's car, side-stepping some puddles in the sidewalks as they went, Gene was very careful to keep his shoes from getting muddy. Even though the dormitory they were interested in was nearby, Gene wanted to take the car to minimize the possibility of mud on his clothes. Ron was able to park almost in front and let Gene access a sidewalk.

In the main lobby of the dormitory, Gene asked a student if she could tell him where Audrey's room was in the dormitory. He got a frowning look and he was asked why he needed that information. He and Ron showed their badges and the student was somewhat mollified. She said she would notify Audrey and went up the stairs.

"Well, that's a little different from when we went to see Roxanne, huh?" Gene commented to Ron.

"It's probably because you look like someone who shouldn't be here, what with your suit all wet and baggy like that," Ron remarked to his colleague. At the same time, Looney thought to himself that he appreciated the self-imposed restriction of not allowing men into this woman's dorm.

Gene quickly brushed his pants and tried to sharpen the creases before he realized his partner was not serious.

"I guess there's different rules in each dorm. Whatever."

Audrey sent word and agreed to meet them in a lounge area just off the lobby on the first floor. The first young woman directed them there and suggested they sit at one of the tables. They only had to wait a few minutes before Audrey joined them. She was a stout girl, about 5 foot eight or nine inches with a regal way of walking. Her short dark hair was cut pixie-like and accentuated her bright blue eyes. Consistent with her majestic behavior, she nodded to them as she entered the room; both felt it appropriate to stand as she approached. As she took her seat she made eye contact with both of them and asked, "How can I help you gentlemen? Are you here about Peggy?"

Ron answered, "Yes, we are. I assume you know what happened?"

"I certainly do not know. But I am aware that she is dead."

"I see," Ron replied, thinking that she had not fallen for his little trick question. "Are you aware of how she died?"

"No. But I am aware that there is some concern about murder," Audrey stated with a air of confidence.

Ron was slightly taken aback but showed only an interest in the source of that information. "Do you mind telling me how you heard that information?" he pressed.

"Not at all. It came from several sources who observed the police and the medical examiner and detectives sniffing around her body."

"I see," Ron said again. "Well, we are investigating what does appear to be a homicide. We were referred to you as someone who might know helpful information about Margaret."

Audrey nodded solemnly and said, "Yes. I probably knew her better than anyone. She was interested in theatre and so am I. Even though she was a sophomore she was good and showed a lot of talent. I'm a senior and well entrenched in this theatre group and I agreed to help her, if I could."

"What did that help look like?" Gene inquired.

"Mostly just talking with her about the mechanics of try-outs, how to work a proscenium stage, being certain she projects her voice, things like that."

"Sounds rather clinical," Ron said

"Well we also spent time together over coffee after rehearsals."

"Did she tell you anything about men in her life?" This was from Gene.

"Right to the point, eh? Sure, she mentioned some things but she was never specific. We had several discussions about goals in her life and particularly what part the theatre might play."

"What can you tell us about a guy? A guy that she was recently seeing," Gene asked.

"We talked about her future, the ideal husband, potential careers and all that. She started dating some guy recently but didn't tell me anything other than she always called him 'my guy'. She said they usually went for pizza and he once took her to his place. She said she didn't think he was marriage material and she said it was all 'just for fun', right now."

"Do you think this guy was a student?"

"No, I'm fairly certain he was not. Something about his 'work' and her class schedule made it necessary for them to meet late at night."

Ron read the indifference in Audrey's voice and recognized the conversation was coming to an end, at least on her end. He thanked her for her help as they stood to go and she gave a slight hint at a courtesy before turning back to the stairs.

Gene said, quietly "Don't think I've ever had an audience with a material witness before."

As they walked back toward where Ron had parked his car, he got a text message.

"OK," he said to Gene, quickening his pace. "The parents are in to claim the body. I told them we would meet when they came to town. We can meet with them now down at the station."

Chapter 13

The Kuykendahls were each approaching fifty and, under other circumstances probably would have appeared as a healthy and contented couple. Mr. Kuykendahl was about five foot eight inches with a broad and deep chest, shoulders to match, topped by a squarish head covered with dark hair streaked in gray. Mrs. Kuykendahl was a few inches shorter with a smaller frame but tending toward matronly. But they were not contented and did not appear healthy, they looked more as if someone had removed a quarter of their body volume; they were slumped and bent, head down and downcast eyes, reddened from crying.

"Mr. & Mrs. Kuykendahl, I'm Detective Looney and this is my partner Detective Novalchek. I'm very sorry for your loss."

They nodded.

"Is there anything I could get for you right now? Coffee? Water?"

They shook their heads.

"I know this is a difficult time. But we need to ask some questions so we can find out what happened."

"Do you have any idea who killed her, detective?" Mr. Kuykendahl was having difficulty keeping his eyes from watering.

"No, sir, we do not," answered Ron. "We actually have very little information to go on and perhaps you can help."

"What can we do?"

"Can you tell me anything about her friends here in Cincinnati? Any boyfriends in particular?"

"She didn't seem to have a lot of friends," her mother murmured. "We talked about once a week but it was mostly about her classes. She didn't say anything about boys."

"Was that unusual for her?," asked Gene. When the Kuykendahls looked at him puzzled by the question, he went on, "Did she have boyfriends in high school?"

"Yes. A couple." Her mother suppressed a sob. "She wasn't big in the dating scene."

"Did she get along well?"

"Oh yes," her father interposed. "Everybody liked her, very popular in high school. She had lots of friends."

Ron asked, "Do you know any of her friends here at the University?"

The Kuykendahls were quiet for a few moments and then each slowly shook their head. They had no idea what their daughter had been doing other than her classwork in Cincinnati.

*　　*　　*

Ron was at his desk. He leaned back in his chair and rubbed his face.

"Gene, we need to go back to the beginning. We haven't found any thread to follow at the end of the story."

"Agreed. The earliest we can document comes at the end of the story is that she was sitting at the park bench on campus at midnight."

"Let's start there. How did she get there? Where was she before that? Do we even feel certain that she was alive when she got to the little park area?"

"The doc didn't say anything about the lividity being different from her sitting where she was killed," Gene offered, leaning back in his chair also.

"Right. OK. Let's take that as a key known. She was alive at the park bench around midnight. How did she get there?" Ron started rustling around in one of the drawers in his desk.

"Whatcha looking for?"

"A map of that part of town."

Just then there was some loud discussion from the other side of the Dick Pen, that quarter of the fourth floor of the Police Building where the Detective Bureau was housed. Gene left Ron to his map search and went to determine the cause of the ruckus. Ron found a city map he was looking for and spread it out on his desk. He marked the area where Margaret's body had been found with a heavy snow globe and was studying the adjacent areas when Gene returned. "What was that all about?" he asked.

Gene shook his head, "They're trying to figure out who's going on a call to the ball park. Somebody thinks there's a DB around the back. Jim-Bob's opinion is it's another sleeping bum. But the real fun is hearing what's going on elsewhere."

"Yeah, what's that?" Ron asked indifferently.

"Two cars collided at the entrance to Bailey Bridge downtown and one guy jumped out and took a machete to the other guy's tires."

"Machete? That's harsh."

"And when the guy tried to stop him, he lopped off the guy's arm!"

"And we thought we had it bad." Ron said, trying to both sound interested while giving most of his attention to the map on his desk.

"Plus Rocky says somebody carjacked a robovan."

Ron finally looked up. "What's a robovan?"

"One of those self driving vehicles. Big companies are using them to deliver stuff and save on drivers."

"Not aware of that. But unless we can get somewhere on this case, Thor may be looking for some robocops." Ron paused for a second and then indicated his map. "Look. Here's where Margaret was found and there's two ways she would have walked to where she was on campus and both ways lead out to housing neighborhoods."

"So, you're thinking she was with somebody who lives off campus?"

"Right. And this guy is walking her home at midnight."

"Is that a 'known'?" Gene asked skeptically.

"Well, not actually," Ron agreed, "But I'd like to think of it as highly probable. Besides what are the alternatives?"

"What about the obvious. She was driven home. I don't see the compelling reason to believe someone was walking her home."

Ron rubbed his chin and inquired, "Just to extend the question and answer, period who would that be?"

Pausing before answering, Gene offered, "Same as before I guess. She knows the guy or she doesn't."

"And if she doesn't know him, why let him get behind her?"

Ron nodded, "Or get in a car with him at midnight. I say we should throw that one out, then. Let's work on the concept that she knew him."

"I agree. I also think the idea that she would let someone she knew but just met, get behind her like that," Ron went on. "I think our best scenario is she knew the guy and walked there with him."

"He walked her home from wherever, before he kills her."

"Also right. Since the roommate was home that night we can guess they weren't at her place. So they must have been at his. In one of these neighborhoods."

"Lot of footwork to cover that big an area looking for a ghost."

"Right again, Gene. That's three in a row. Plus I'm guessing we can't rely on a lot of uniforms to help with all the other protest stuff going on downtown."

"So what's the play, partner?"

"I think we should begin closer to the end. Let's walk the main streets looking for some place where she would've gotten that coffee she had late at night and just before death."

"Asking if they've seen the girl in our pictures."

"Gene, that's a whole lotta 'rights' in a row. You're on some kinda roll."

CHAPTER 14

The following morning Ron and Gene began the tedious task of walking the street and looking for any indication of the prior presence of Margaret Kuykendahl. Using the copy of the class photo from the yearbook, they stopped at several different stores and coffee shops asking for information. At midnight all of the stores were closed and none had surveillance cameras.

They tried three coffee shops but the owners and baristas there indicated that their shop usually closed by nine o'clock. Gene was getting discouraged and suggested Peggy might have had the coffee at "her man's" house before starting the walk home.

And, that's if she even did walk home," he said, more under his breath than Ron could hear. Ron was also becoming disenchanted with the theory as he recognized the pattern of coffee shops closing well before midnight. Then, they found an outlier at the fourth shop. The sign on the door denoted an opening time of four in the afternoon with late closing around midnight. As they stood in front of the coffee shop shortly after one in the afternoon, Ron wanted to get a high-five from his partner; instead they made plans to circle back later.

Gene said, "You know we are almost into the neighborhood here, why don't we go try the other route?"

Ron smiled, "You really are on a roll. I thought you were about to chuck it in."

They walked back to the small park on the campus, timing their stroll and then took a right angle and again began canvassing the shops and the single coffee shop they could identify on that route. By four-thirty that afternoon they had exhausted all possibilities on the second route and found themselves back at the small park area.

"I'm ready for some food," Gene said, sitting at the park bench. "I feel like we've been at this for weeks."

"Huh. I thought you would have gained an appreciation of why I like to walk the area."

"Yeah, not so much. And I only got that 'play' sandwich back around noon. I'm hungry."

"No time to visit Sandra right now, pal. We've got one more stop before we call it a day."

"All right. But could we drive there?"

"Sure."

The late-opening coffee shop was not particularly busy; only two customers were sitting at the tables when they entered. The owner looked up and asked, "What can I get you gentlemen?"

"Steak and baked potato," Gene cracked.

"Long day, is it?" the owner rejoined. "I can get you some specialty coffee but we don't have the kitchen for steaks."

"Two coffees would be great," Ron opined. "And some information." He flashed his badge and the owner nodded before busying himself with drawing two small coffees.

They sat at one of the small tables in front of the counter with the owner, introduced themselves and got his name, Bernard Fleming. Ron asked, "If you would, we'd like to ask some questions about late night customers."

Fleming agreed, so Ron showed him the yearbook picture of Margaret. His response was straightforward and prompt.

"Yeah, she was in here. Couple of nights ago."

'What time?"

"Late, I guess. I think I was about to close when she came in."

"So that would be about what, midnight?"

"Yeah, about that.

"Was she alone?" Ron asked.

"No. There was a guy with her."

Both detectives sat up and became much more interested in the answers. Ron took out his small pad and favorite pen to annotate the description.

"What did he look like, then?"

"I really didn't see him so much. I mean, they came in the front here and she came to the counter to order. He just kept going and went to the back tables over there," the owner indicated the tables to the left and around the corner from the counter. "I didn't actually see him after that."

"Why was that?" both detectives asked.

"Well, he was back there where I couldn't see him from the counter. This girl paid for their drinks and took them to one of those tables where he was sitting. And a little later, I was in the back packing up stuff preparing to close and they went out the door. The little bell told me someone had opened the door. I came out in case it was a late customer but it was just them leaving."

"Can you describe him?'

"I don't know. I didn't really get a look at him so much."

"Try to remember, please. White or black?"

"Pretty sure he was white."

"How tall was he?"

"OK. Well, when they came in the door they looked about the same height. Came right to the level of the words painted on the door, see?" He pointed to the shop's name lettered on the front glass door.

"What was he wearing?" pressed Ron.

"Uh, I think it was something like a jacket, maybe military? And a baseball cap?"

"Any logo on the cap?"

"I don't think so. It was just a dark cap."

"How about the jacket? Any patches or anything on it?"

"I don't remember any. But, look, I didn't really pay much attention to him. She was asking me for their drinks.

"What did they order?"

"A medium latte and an Americano."

"Anything to eat?"

"No just the drinks."

Gene looked up and asked, "How long were they here?"

The owner thought for a second then replied, "Couldn't have been long, I was about to close before they came in and they left soon after while I was packing stuff in the back."

"So what time do you think they actually left?"

"Musta been right about midnight, I guess."

"I guess you don't have a surveillance camera, do you?"

"Nope. Too costly."

"Would you sit with one of our artists and help us get a Rembrandt of the guy?"

"Yeah, I guess so. But I've told you what I remember."

Nonetheless, and remembering that witness recall increases over a day or so before it deteriorates into confabulation, the detectives pushed Bernard ('Please call me Bernie') to accept the challenge of meeting the police artist to make a drawing of the man he briefly saw with Margaret just before she was killed. He asked them for an afternoon appointment and they agreed to work with the artist on scheduling.

Afterward, sitting in Ron's car near the coffee shop, Gene said, "I think this is the best we're gonna do. Average height, white guy, army jacket and baseball cap."

Ron replied, "I think we're back out here tomorrow looking for surveillance cameras on this route. We're gonna need more'n that vague description to start looking for a guy in the neighborhood. And besides, Bernie agreed to work with Ashley on a drawing, and you know how good she is at getting people to remember things."

CHAPTER 15

Confident that they knew the path of the couple toward the University campus, Ron and Gene started the next day driving that route slowly and looking for security cameras. Once again they were in Ron's car but with little criticism from Gene. They cruised the major routes away from the campus that led into neighborhoods, University Avenue heading east and Jefferson Avenue heading south. Ron drove leisurely in the right hand lane looking at the buildings on the left while Gene in the passenger seat paid attention to the right side of the street.

Two of the retail stores on the Jefferson route did have video surveillance that covered their front doors and which might have shown the sidewalk but both stores turned the cameras off at closing time. There were no parking areas on the street that might have been covered and a couple hours of surveying the rooftops and telephone poles on the route were fruitless.

Ron said, "OK, I'm tired of looking up and getting a crick in my neck."

"Me too. Wanna get something to eat?"

"Not just yet. I have another idea."

Accordingly, they made passes up and down University without finding anything different until Ron suggested they disregard telephone poles and external building entrances. Not long after that they found what Ron had been looking for. There was an ATM machine facing the street inside a small glassed in foyer along the route. Ron parked nearby and used his card to enter the small enclosure. From that advantage the detectives examined the sightlines. The probable camera angle might give them a view of the street for perhaps half a block on the other side. However, they also knew this was going to be helpful only if the camera was one of the 24/7 type.

Ron was not able to convince his partner to delay lunch any longer, so they drove to Sandy's work place and had the 'usual' with another round of smiles and delayed leaving. Gene seemed more focused after he was able to get a 'usual' and he and Ron settled in with the security officer from the bank and began reviewing tapes.

"You're lucky to have called us today," the officer said. "I likely would have erased these files sometime soon."

"Really?" Ron asked. "I thought memory was cheap enough for you to keep the videos forever."

"Well, it is cheap," the officer allowed, "but it still costs something and we don't find a use for these videos after about a month or so."

"Still, you've got the one we want from the angle we want."

"If it makes you happy, then we're happy, too."

Honing down their time frame to begin at ten p.m. on the day in question, Ron and Gene sat at the monitor in the security office and allowed the tape to run in double time. As expected, the film was mostly void of activity, simply showing the street view with an occasional passing car.

"Wait. Stop. That's it," Ron said excitedly. "Back it up."

On replay they could see the far side of the street and a couple of storefronts. As they replayed the critical portion they saw two figures walk into view. The couple, man and woman, were holding hands with the man walking on the curbside. The couple appeared to be nearly the same height. The man was limping and wearing a baseball cap and what appeared to be a military jacket. He was turned mostly toward the woman and away from the camera for the quarter of a block that was caught on camera.

"Can't see his face!" Ron said with disappointment.

"That jacket does kinda look like an army jacket," Gene offered.

"We will need to take a copy of this video," Ron mentioned to the security officer who promptly nodded and began making a copy.

"Maybe we can get the guys in IT to enhance this and get some facial rec," Ron went on. He turned to the security officer and said, "Hold on to that one, will you? I want to be sure we can get something off the copy before we lose the original."

The officer nodded.

"You notice that funny way he's walking? Consistent limp." Gene was still focusing on the screen.

"Yeah. What're you thinking, Gene?"

"Well, Army jacket and a limp could be a veteran. Maybe even one getting physical therapy."

"Good idea. We can go check on that right after taking this video down to IT."

CHAPTER 16

R on approached Harold Tinney, the departmental Information Technologist in Harold's office in the basement of Police Headquarters.

"Hey, Harold. You tired of the old guys calling you 'cause they can't figger out their email?"

Harold looked up and showed a tight grin. "It keeps me employed, Walker. I like to eat."

Harold was not telling a secret about his propensity for food. He was known to make every division party and obtain a heaping plate of food. At nearly 300 pounds, Harold couldn't conceal his love of food if he tried. He was 5-foot 8 inches in height and close to that in girth; his work uniform was overalls and a long-sleeved T-shirt. His face was always happy, however, with or without the thick glasses he wore for his near-sightedness. Harold was also known to always have the exact tool needed to work on anyone's computer because he kept a wide array of screwdrivers and other devices in the bib of the overalls.

He asked, "You come for lunch or for a favor?"

Ron responded, "How about some diverting work of high importance."

"If you expect me to respond to additional work with enthusiasm and glee, you'll need to give me a minute to work up an act."

"Tell me when you're ready. I've got a possible murderer on tape and need better facial recognition."

"C'mon now, Walker. Don't underplay your hand like that. Promise me a Subway sandwich for a favor. Act like you care."

"Oh, I care, Harold. And I'd be happy to get you a sandwich but this is no favor, it's real life homicide detecting."

"Make it the Italian Hero. Footlong."

"Deal. Why do I always feel like I should have brought a menu when I come down here?"

"Beats me. Must be the long journey down to the basement of the world that makes you think of food."

"Right. Look here's the tape from the bank on University. I need a better picture of the guy." Ron went on to specify the time stamp that showed the man and woman walking. Harold said he would get to it right away and Ron headed for the door. He was stopped by a loud cry.

"Aw no." Harold said. "This may cost you several Subways."

"What are you talking about?" Ron inquired as he returned to the desk where Harold was turning the tape over in his hands.

"This is one of those multiple re-use tapes from an ATM, isn't it?"

"Yeah. I said it was from a bank."

"Well, banks have lots of different security feeds and tapes. And this is one of the worst."

"Why's that?'

"Two big reasons. First is the re-use. Over time the tapes become fatigued and lose their ability to hold an image. But that's not the big one here. The other reason is it's analog."

"And that's bad because . . .?"

"Man, you got no business making fun of the guys that can't load their email if you don't know the difference between analog and digital," Harold said this pulling himself up straight in his chair.

"Watch it, man. That Subway may just turn out to be six inches."

"Analog sucks for what you want, Walker. I'm just guessing here but the picture you need enhanced is not someone sticking their face up to the camera, right?"

"Yeah, that's right. The picture we're interested in does not involve our prep sticking his face up to the camera. I' homicide, remember, not Bank Robbery."

"Banks don't really much care about anything unless it's close to the camera, so they always go cheap on the ATMs. The analog camera is cheaper than digital and so is the recording unit. Plus, the feed is much easier since it can go over coax cable instead of a LAN."

"I already understood that analog was older and cheaper than digital for cameras and such," Ron said leaning on the desk. "What's that got to do with what I asked you?"

"Let me take another guess. The face of the guy you want enhanced for facial rec is on a guy walking by on the street."

Ron nodded. "Actually on the other side of the street."

"Even better!" Harold said sarcastically, throwing his hands in the air. "The image quality on the best analog camera is pretty low to start with. And banks don't get the best to start with. The resolution is pretty crappy unless the subject is up close. Now when you start looking across the street everything will be blurry and grainy. You're looking for a miracle here."

"Yeah, OK. You're our miracle worker. Just get it done," Ron said turning back toward the door. "Zoom in and do the best you can."

His comment was greeted by hooting laughter. He turned back and asked, "OK. What did I just say that would draw such cackling derision?"

Harold looked at him for a moment and explained like he was talking to a child, " You can't 'zoom' an analog film. Things just get more grainy and indistinct. I thought you knew that much."

Ron's shoulders slumped and after a moment he asked, "Please see what you can do and at least get me a disc with the short segment on it with the two of them walking. Is that possible?"

Harold nodded solemnly then showed a smirk, "I'll have your request done in the morning, Walker. Will you be by before lunch?"

Ron took a deep breath and said, "Of course, with a foot-long Italian sandwich."

CHAPTER 17

"Coffee?"

"You mean on the way back to the office?"

"Exactly. At this time of day, the pot up there is either empty or you wish it was."

"Let's go," Ron said. They exited the side entrance and headed down the block toward their favorite coffee shop.

With their cups full and the day about to finish, they sat in the rear of the shop. Gene took a first sip and asked, "So, the Reds are back from Spring Training. They looked pretty good down there. You think they'll make the playoffs this year?"

"You got tickets or something, Gene? Like that basketball tournament?"

"Too early for that. I'm just wondering if you think they'll make it this year."

"Why don't you ask me again in a couple of months?" Ron said with a small smirk as he sipped his cup.

"OK, I will, smart guy. But why wait till then? Don't you have any ideas now?" Gene goaded.

"From what I read and what I saw in the couple of games I watched on Spring Ball, the starters seem solid but not overwhelming. I mean there's no Cy Young in the group." He paused and stopped Gene from speaking by raising his hand. "At the same time, the pen looks weak."

"Everybody in the division has a weak pen, you know that."

"Maybe. At this point every team's pen is a little suspect. Until it's not, and they slam the door on league leaders three times in a row. All I'm saying is that it's just up in the air right now. But ask me again in two months; I'll have an answer for you then."

"C'mon, partner, what's so magic about two months?"

"Statistics. Except for really bizarre accidents like the Nationals starting off 19-31 and still winning the Series, most every year, teams pretty much finish where they are on the first of June."

"You're making that up!" Gene said.

"Am not. Look it up. That's probably why the league was able to settle on a 60-game season during the COVID thing."

Gene sat back in his chair. He knew his partner was not deeply engaged in sports; no favorite teams and often doing something other than watching games on Saturday and Sunday afternoons. Except for that habit of always knowing what was going on with the Razorbacks. That seeming disinterest had led Gene to believe that an in-depth discussion of baseball between them was unlikely. Now Ron turns out to have something that sounds like inside information about the sport going back many years. He decided to change the subject and return to baseball when he had a chance to determine the validity of Ron's claim concerning the first of June.

"Seems like we have a couple of 'Knowns' here," Gene offered.

"Right. I see them as: One, they were together most likely at his place earlier. Two, he walked her back to campus and they stopped and had coffee on the way. Three, he killed her in the little park."

Gene held up a hand. "Can we say it's a 'Known' that he killed her? I mean he could have left her at the campus and she encountered someone else walking to her dormitory."

Ron thought about this and replied, "You may be right about that not being a 'Known' but I'm gonna keep it as a Most Probable."

"I can agree with that."

"So, what would flip the scene from casual evening together to murder at the end?"

"How about the usual difference between Mars and Venus?"

"Meaning?"

"She wants more from the relationship and he's just playing it for the moment."

Ron wrinkled his nose. "That doesn't agree with what that Audrey told us about Margaret saying this was 'all for fun'."

"Uh huh. But that was some time ago. She also said 'right now'. Maybe something had changed."

"Wouldn't that lead to an argument first? Not even veterans jump from 'I don't like what you said' to 'I'm gonna kill you' in one step."

"No. I mean they are discussing it all along." After this comment, Gene paused and looked down in his cup. He and Ron both thought through this possibility for a minute or two.

"The hand holding on the video doesn't look like an argument." Ron finally said, with a small frown.

"Well, there is that."

"And there's no evidence at post that they fought. No defensive bruises or anything. She let the killer get behind her and put his arms around her," Ron went on, gaining enthusiasm for refuting the quarrel concept.

"OK. OK." Gene said, signaling surrender of the idea. "You got another idea?"

"Not right now. But the video makes me think something went on after they left the coffee shop. Maybe she heard something or saw something he didn't want her to know."

"And she still lets him get behind her?"

"Yeah, OK. That doesn't make sense either." After this admission Ron's frown became deeper and he sat back in his chair to think.

After a moment of silence, Gene took up the idea himself. "Unless she didn't know that she had seen something important."

"Possible," Ron agreed. "We're not likely to tease that out until after we get this guy."

"Back to the 'Knowns'. They were probably coming from his place in that neighborhood. We need to spend some time in there knocking on doors."

"I agree but we need more than the sketchy idea of a army jacket and baseball cap. Tinney says we'll not get anything helpful in way of close up or facial rec from that analog tape. We need to get something to show to people about this guy. That coffee shop is about to open again. Let's get the Bernie and Ashley to agree on a time as soon as possible for the two of them to sit downand try to get us some kind of a picture."

CHAPTER 18

Bernie Fleming was a night owl. After he closed his coffee ship at midnight he often went to the Waffle House on McMillan for breakfast before heading to his home in Clifton Heights. At home he would feed the cat, clean out the litter box and make himself a drink of milk and Bailey's Irish Cream over ice. He sat in his big overstuffed chair in the den, sipped his drink and read for another hour or so before going to bed. As a result of his schedule, Bernie was not eager to make an arrangement for an early morning appointment with the police artist.

After some negotiation between Bernie and the artist, a young woman from the University Art Department who was working for the police as a consultant, Ron was able to get them to agree on an early afternoon appointment for the drawing. Bernie was a little late but he brought coffee for himself and the artist and smoothed over the somewhat uneven start.

Using the usual techniques the artist was able to tease out of Bernie some remembrance of the shape of the perpetrator's facial structure, brows, nose eyes and chin and went to work on her computer with various templates. The two of them developed a friendly repartee as they conspired to get a digital image that Bernie thought was close to his fleeting memory of the man in question.

Perhaps Bernie's indecision slowed the process but Ron thought Bernie was stretching the process out because he enjoyed the close company of the young woman artist. Nonetheless, he did not interrupt the work. As the time for Bernie's shop to open grew closer, the process came to an end and Bernie agreed the picture they had created was as good and as close to his memory as could be expected.

"Thank you for your help, Mr. Fleming," Ron said, shaking the man's hand as he walked him to the exit.

"Not at all. Actually sort of enjoyable," he replied.

Ron gave Fleming his card and asked him to call if he remembered anything else about the couple.

Ron and Gene then sat with the artist and looked at the digital picture. Gene finally asked, "Isn't this pretty much what you two had agreed on about an hour ago?" He smiled at the artist.

"Yes, but he wanted to try some other features to see if he would change his mind," she countered.

Ron noted, "He's twice your age, Ashley. Don't you think you could have finished a little earlier?"

"Hey, he was sweet. And he brought me coffee. You never do that. You got what you wanted."

"And you got an extra hour of consultant fees, eh?"

"Clearly a win-win for everyone here, guys."

"Well, before you hit the print button," Ron asked, "Would you do something for us? I'd like a picture with a beard, too. I think it's possible this guy has been around and may have changed his appearance."

Ashley nodded and asked, "Beard? You want full, short, goatee, Van Dyke, what?"

Ron smiled at her, "C'mon Ashley. I'll bring you coffee the next time I call you. Put the right beard on him, OK?"

"Sure, boss. Right away, boss." She turned to her work and said clearly, "Two sugars."

CHAPTER 19

Ron earned the name 'Walker' by walking the full extent of the patrol area he was assigned in his early days with the force. Growing up on a farm in rural Arkansas, Ron had been assigned outdoor chores from the time he could read. Plus, he and his father and brother were hunters and by the time he left home for the military at age 18, Ron had walked all over his south Arkansas county, uphill, downhill, through brush and across creeks. His stride was easy and light and did not tire him. Ron explained he felt more attuned to the environment when he was outside as opposed to sitting in a patrol car. Not that he was contrary to riding in a car as a detective, but the walking to knock doors and interview people made him feel more engaged in the hunt for a killer than pursuing internet leads.

Gene Novalchek was not as proficient or comfortable as Ron Looney in walking a beat. He was, on the other hand, physically fit from his boxing days. He remained at a stable weight, in spite of seeming to constantly be looking to the next meal, and easily passed the physical requirements for detective every year. But he broke into a sweat fairly easily and walking several blocks in non-air conditioned temperatures regularly put large circles under his arms. Gene was very aware of the effect this would have not only on interviewees but also on his expensive suits. So his 'walk' was always slower than Ron's, more liable to keep within shady areas and generally accomplished without his jacket.

They had divided the area to be covered by the simple expedient of each taking one side of the street between blocks. Their different styles actually allowed them to cover more ground in a given amount of time even though they always remained within each other's sight. Partly to compensate for his slower pace, Gene tended to cut across lawns from one front porch to the next whenever the landscape allowed. Those occasions when the property line was defined by flower beds or a fence caused him to go around and added more steps for him. Ron, however, was respectful of the lawns he was assigned; he remained on the sidewalk up and down the street and up to each house.

At the end of each block the first interviewer to complete his assignment would wait for the other to catch up before they started on the next block. This also allowed a short break-always in the shade-to discuss findings to that point. Ron was usually the first to complete his task and Gene occasionally asked, "How many people did you talk to, anyway?" with the clear implication that Ron was doing less work.

Ron's answer usually was that only one of the houses had no response to his knock and, he enjoyed telling his partner, he had enjoyable discussions with other homeowners about their flowerbeds.

Gene knew his partner was truly in his element when he could walk a beat, stop and chat with civilians and discuss issues of shared concern that had nothing to do with homicide. But that wasn't what they were walking this neighborhood to discuss. He determined he would talk faster because he was already walking as fast as he wanted to go.

Chapter 20

On the third day of their canvassing the neighborhood, Gene asked Ron at the second corner stop, "Are you real certain we can't get some uniforms down here to help with this?"

"Didn't ask today, but Thor said no with both his mouth and his eyes yesterday."

"We've covered nearly thirty blocks in this area. Are you sure we're in the right place?"

"You saw the map. This is the most likely area, but there's still another whole neighborhood out the other way."

"My shoes are getting tight."

"Yeah, this is unusual activity for you. Maybe you could put on some gloves and dance around and your feet would feel better."

"I actually did some dancing last night."

"With Sandy?"

"Of course. But maybe that's why you get so far ahead of me. I have a social life that uses up some of my energy."

"Get your social dancing down this block. Another hour and we'll get the car and go see Sandy. I'm really getting hooked on the 'usual.'"

They covered two more blocks before stopping for lunch. Ron parked near the diner where Sandy worked and commented to Gene as they walked to the shop, "You look like you regained your strength, there."

"C'mon, man, I'm not about to go in there limping after a big night out dancing. You know I can't do that."

"So, you can limp with me but not with her?"

"Well, . . ."

"I was gonna say that hurts my feelings but as I think about it, that means we're a lot more honest with each other doesn't it?" He noted Gene's head nodding and hurriedly went on, "And that makes me feel so good about our friendship that I wouldn't even think about mentioning your fatigue and whining about walking today when she comes to the table."

"Great."

"Oh, and I don't have any hard feelings about you paying for my lunch, either."

"Rat fink!"

"Now I know we're close. That's what my brother used to call me." Ron opened the door for Gene and ostentatiously waved him in.

Somewhere in the mid-afternoon Gene found a man working in his yard who had something to say about the picture they were showing around. Gene called for Ron to join him. Ron excused himself from a discussion on the other side of the street and crossed over.

Gene made quick introductions. "Mr. Garing, this is my partner, Ron Looney. Please tell us about seeing this man."

Ron stuck out his hand and the man shook it. Garing was a frail man, stooped and with little meat on his frame and his hair was sparse and gray and present only on the edges of his head. "Well, like I told you. He come around here looking to rent my 'partment." Garing's voice was a little raspy and Ron thought it was from years of smoking.

"Do you know his name?"

"He maybe said it but I don't remember."

"Are you sure this is the same man?"

"Well, kinda. I mean, it was 4 months ago and I ain't seen him since. But that's looks kinda like him."

"And did you rent to him?"

"Sure did."

"Is the apartment here?"

"Yep. I call it a garage 'partment, but there's no garage. It's right back here," he said as he slowly led the detectives to the rear of his house down a narrow drive way.

In the back of the house was a small building, scarcely wider than the driveway but much longer. The building had likely been a garage in a former time, when cars were not very wide. The front had a single door and window and there did not appear to be windows on the sides.

Ron stepped to the door and knocked but received no answer. Gene peered through the window and shook his head.

Ron turned back to the owner of the apartment. "Have you seen this man recently?"

"Nah. He pays his rent in cash. Ever' month he puts an envelope in my mailbox with the money in it. I ain't seen him since he took the place."

"Why is that?" Gene pushed. "Seems like he can't walk to the street without passing by your windows."

"Well, I don't know, I guess. It's just what happened. I'm all retired here. I don't go out much, 'cept to get groceries or stuff. Mostly I sleep upstairs and watch TV."

"Do you have any idea where he may be now?"

"Not really."

"Does he ever have other people over?"

"Not that I know's of."

"Could he be a student?"

"Maybe. He looked kinda older than that, though."

"Do you have any idea when he might be back?"

"Nope. He pretty much comes and goes without me seeing him."

"Would you look at this picture again? Are you certain this is the man you rented your apartment to?"

Garing took a moment or two to carefully examine the drawings Ron held in front of him. "Yeah, it looks like him. The one without the beard anyway."

"Thank you Mr. Garing. That's all for now," Ron said as he started back out the driveway.

He and Gene huddled at the street to discuss their situation.

"Is this enough?" Gene asked.

"Depends on what we are aiming for, I guess."

"And what are we aiming for?"

"Good enough reason to suspect our killer rented a place."

"Are we stopping the search, then?" Gene asked hopefully.

"We probably shouldn't since we've only covered about twenty percent of the area we sketched out. But we were likely to stop when we got a hit anyway."

"If you consider his identification to be a 'hit'."

"From a drawing taken from a poor witness and him having to recall what he saw four months ago, yes, I'll take that."

"Then what's the next move?"

"Stake out. We'll get some help and spend the next few days watching for this guy to come back. And when he does, we should have our guy."

CHAPTER 21

R on had visited New City Hospital several times in the past year, almost always to see and visit with his old friend, Tom Bolling. Tom was a retired Air Force brigadier general, an orthopedic surgeon and chief of staff at the Hospital. Ron and Tom had a long-standing friendship that dated back to earlier days when they were both in uniform. On a couple of occasions Ron had helped Tom handle tricky cases of murder in the hospital and those cases had started with Tom asking for assistance. Their friendship now included Ron attending Tom's Christmas party for the hospital faculty and Tom and Sandra reciprocating with attendance at Ron's annual Fourth of July barbecue. Consequently, Ron had no compunction about 'turn-about'; he was there to ask Tom to give him some help on the campus murder.

Ron had been to the hospital several times and on many of those occasions gone with Tom to get coffee at the Green Bean kiosk in the lobby. Nonetheless, he was taken a little by surprise when the barista Tom had called Nick caught his eye and asked, "the usual?" As he nodded in response, Ron wondered, 'do I have a 'usual'? and if I do, how does he know it?' As Nick went to work, Ron stepped to the end of the line to pay but when the cashier asked him what he had ordered he had to chuckle. "Nick is making me a 'usual' and I'm waiting to see what that is."

The cashier hollered at Nick who hollered back, "Red Eye" and the cashier took Ron's money. When his cup was placed on the counter, he caught Nick's eye and saluted him with the cup before moving through the lobby to the Executive Suite. As he walked he began to ponder the ways in which his life of chasing criminals and killers had become so predictable that he now regularly ate a 'usual' for lunch and got a 'usual' coffee in the afternoon. He was about to consider that he was becoming someone he did not know and he didn't understand how he got to this point. He wondered how any of his friends would be able to remember him if he changed any more.

Mary Brighthouse remembered him and said, "Detective Looney, how nice to see you. Is Dr. Bolling expecting you?"

"No. I didn't call ahead. I just happened to be nearby and thought I'd drop in. Is that OK?"

"Well, I don't think he has anyone in there right now. Let me see."

She went to the door of Tom's office and knocked. After hearing him, she opened the door and said, "Detective Looney is here to see you."

Mary opened the door wide and indicated for Ron to enter. Tom stood up to greet him saying, "I hope this isn't something bad I don't know about."

"No, no. Not at all. I was just nearby and I have a question."

"Or did you come for the coffee? I see you took time to stop by the Green Bean."

"Yeah. And Nick thinks I have a 'usual'."

"What did he make you?"

"A Red Eye."

"Good drink for this time of day. He makes me a Black Eye every morning."

"Well, us flyboys gotta stick together, right?"

"Absolutely. So how can I help?"

"I've got a case that's got me hung up right now and I'd like to talk about it a bit."

Tom indicated for Ron to sit in the overstuffed chair in front of his desk and he returned to his desk chair. "Go ahead. My schedule is clear for the rest of the day."

And Ron talked, in medium deep detail. Tom was generally quiet but now and again made appropriate noises and head gestures to indicate his discomfort with the death of a young girl and particularly with her method of dying.

"I think you're right about that," he said when Ron mentioned that the M.E. had suspicion that the death was from a neck snap. Ron was surprised to learn that Tom had spent a few months at Elgin Air Base in Florida early in his career to help train some of the medical personnel in the Ranger education program in injury prevention. Tom said, "I did not ever actually see a neck snap but I did see a couple of men who injured their neck. And I did go over the mechanics of the snap with the trainers. This really does sound like it."

"That's what I thought, too. Which leaves me chasing a military trained killer."

"Why come to me?" Tom asked reasonably. "How do you think I can help? Do you want me to teach you how to do it?"

"No, thanks, sensei." Ron made a bowing motion toward Tom. "Fact is, Gene and I have found what we think is a video of the guy and this Margaret girl walking toward the Cincy campus and he has a limp."

"And my original question still stands. Why does that make you think of me?"

"Well, what we originally thought was 'vet with a bum wheel'. Then we wondered if maybe he was doing some rehab. You know those Special Ops guys, they want to get back in their unit ASAP."

"Yes. OK. So?"

"So I spent the day at the VA and they don't know the guy. All I've got is a drawing from the coffee shop owner who admits he didn't see the fella very well and a long range video of him walking about a quarter of a block."

"What do you need?"

"I want a name. I think we have identified where he rented a place near campus and we've got eyes on it, but he's been a no show for a couple of days and we think he may have flown."

Tom took a deep breath, leaned forward, slowly asked, "And you think I can help because. . .?"

"You've got a Nationally Ranked Physical Rehabilitation program here at New City. He may be one of your patients, even if he is a veteran. I'd like to show your therapists this drawing and maybe get someone to look at the video and see if it rings any bells."

Tom paused for a moment before saying, "I don't think our therapists will be as keen to help you as am I."

"Is this a 'police are bad' thing with your therapists?"

"No. At least that's not what I'm thinking. It's more about privacy and confidentiality."

"Even if they know it's a case of murder?"

"I'm not certain that would be persuasive coming from you, as someone who stands to benefit from their information."

Ron sat up straight in the chair, he blinked several times and his nostrils flared. Tom watched as Ron reacted to the perceived insult. When he spoke there was some grittiness in his voice, "You know, Tom, there's probably some way I could subpoena someone to tell me whether this guy has been here."

Tom shook his head quietly and commented, "That's a lot of somebodies looking for something or someone. Could you be more specific, detective?"

Ron heard the questioning voice of a judge, sitting in judgment on Ron's theoretical subpoena or warrant, and he realized Tom was right. Ron knew he and Gene were on the proverbial "fishing trip"; he needed much more specificity for a subpoena and he didn't have any. Moreover, he didn't know where to get it. He made a tight smile at Tom accompanied by a small nod and he leaned back in the chair and

cooled down.

Tom thought about the situation and waved a finger in the air to indicate he was considering how he could help his friend. After a few minutes Tom said, "I tell you what, Ron. These therapists are very good and very protective of their patients. Why don't you let me take the picture and sit with them and see if they are willing to make an identification?"

Ron was a little embarrassed about his threat of legal action and said, "Would you?"

"Sure. I know these therapists very well and they know I respect their relationship with their patients."

"How will you persuade them to identify him?"

"I have my ways, grasshopper. I have my ways.

CHAPTER 22

"Dr. Bolling, is what you are asking us allowed under HIPAA?" asked the chief of physical therapy at New City. "I mean, it does involve PHI." She was referring to personal health information protected under the Health Insurance Portability and Accountability Act.

"Yes, Janice, it is. However, I checked with counsel. No one is trying to get health information in this request. Although what we are asking for is 'personal', meaning a name for a given person, that alone does not come under the rubric of the Act. My friend is just trying to learn this man's name for police reasons."

"What are those reasons?" asked Janice.

"Does that matter?" Tom responded.

"Well . . . we'd just like to know what we're involved in, I think."

Two other therapists nodded vigorously; they wanted to be aware and know what their information was being used for especially if it was to be used against one of their patients. Tom understood their desire to be informed but he also knew that Ron would have dodged the question carefully since the therapists really did not have a 'need to know'. He decided that he would split the difference. He stood up and said, "I have been informed by a highly reliable member of the police department that this information is potentially critical in their approach to a major crime in the city. Even if I knew the specifics of the case under consideration at this point I would not think it appropriate to disclose any more information than that."

Janice also stood, faced Tom and asked, "And you are personally convinced that this information is both critical and not an infraction of the Privacy Act?"

"Yes, I am," Tom was firm and quiet in his pronouncement.

Janice had worked closely with Tom since his arrival at New City. She respected his knowledge about rehabilitation for amputees and had occasionally asked him to talk with some patients for encouragement. More important at this time, however, she recalled the times she had worked in committee assignments where Tom also had a role. She had been surprised at his manner of getting input from everyone and generally making final decisions that everyone could agree with. She thought his leadership was a strength and now she decided that if he were taking this strong a stand in his request, there surely was a right and proper reason for it.

"Well," she said, "if you're sure it's OK. Let's see the drawings."

Tom had several copies of the drawing made before the meeting and he handed the batch to Janice. She opened the folder containing the drawings and began distributing them, one to each therapist.

Tom watched the therapists as the drawings circulated around the group. Most of them bent over the picture and studied it closely; two held their copy up to the light. Tom noticed that one therapist, Rebecca, showed more interest than the others.

"Becca?"

"Well, it's not a terribly close likeness but I think it does look like Thomas Whelan. I've been working with him for a couple of months to regain function after a fractured acetabulum."

"What do you know about him?"

"He was referred from the VA because their hip therapist is off on active duty."

"How did he injure his hip?"

"Something that happened on active duty. We talked about it twice but he was never really clear. I wondered if maybe he also had a head injury and couldn't remember but he laughed and said his head was perfectly fine."

"Why wouldn't he tell you how the injury happened or anything about it? "

"You know the old joke, he said, 'If I tell you I'll have to kill you'. But he was smiling when he said it."

"Did he ever tell you anything more?"

"He once said he was '11B' but I don't know what that means."

"It's pretty general, like an infantryman. What was his story about the hip fracture? I mean what did he *say* happened?"

"I think he said he got hurt in a fall."

"When did you last see him?"

"Maybe a week ago?"

"Did you have a chance to review his x-rays?"

"Not really. He said they were at the VA Medical Center. They sent him over here like I said.. He didn't seem particularly happy about the referral at first but we got over that."

"Does he have scheduled therapy?"

"Yes. I think so. I haven't done a discharge summary on his therapy yet."

"If he shows up for therapy would you please have someone call me right away."

"Yes sir."

Tom addressed the other therapists, "Anyone else see a familiar face on that drawing?"

Some heads went down to re-examine the drawing, others looked at Tom and shook a negative reply. He asked for the drawings back and thanked Janice for arranging the brief meeting before he left.

CHAPTER 23

R on and Gene were taking care of some paper work related to the case when Captain Thorason walked by. "Anything?" he asked in his usual pointed and frugal style.

"We've got some leads, Cap'n."

"Good." Thorason didn't move.

"Ah, we think we've got a likeness for the killer. A coffee shop owner saw him and the girl together shortly before she died."

"Huh." He remained standing and looking at them.

"And, you know we found a probable rental for him and we've got eyes on it."

After another short pause without saying anything, Thorason turned and went back to his office.

"Should we be giving him regular reports?" Gene asked.

"He asks if he wants more information. I doubt he wants extra paper. None of us do. Whether we are writing it or reading it, that usually just takes time away from getting stuff done."

"I know that. But the bosses seem to want that anyway. It's almost like they want to know everything as soon as we do. Without putting in the effort."

"Yeah. But Thor's not that guy. He didn't ask for anything but a quick oral update. And usually when he does that it's because somebody wants to hear from him about progress."

"Maybe he should be pushing for more information on that DB over at the ballpark or that robovan hijacking."

"Why? Something happening on those?"

"I hear the DB is still unidentified but he had been strangled with some kind of cord."

"Garrote."

"Yeah. And they didn't find it and so Jim-Bob are handling a Murder One without a clue."

"They aren't very far behind us, are they?" asked Ron with a slight grin.

His desk phone rang and he picked it up. "Walker"

He listened for a minute and said, "We'll be right over."

"What's up?" Gene asked as Ron got up from his desk.

"Guy over in Narco says he may have seen our guy. Let's go hear his story."

The 'guy in Narco' was Sergeant Harvey Upton, a large black man with a bald head and a thick full beard speckled with grey. He was sitting at his desk and waved Ron and Gene over as they entered the area. He pulled a chair over from his partner's desk and Ron grabbed another from the other side and they sat facing Harvey.

"Haven't seen you around recently, Harv. You been under?" Ron asked, referring to the frequent times narcotics officers spend in some form of undercover operation. The early part of Upton's career had involved undercover and his path had crossed with Ron during that period. They had developed a solid friendship since.

"Nah, man. I got hurt. Jumped off a wall chasing a guy and blew my knee." As he said this he swiveled his right leg out from under the desk to reveal a cumbersome brace.

"Oh man, that's tough. Knees are bad business. You OK now?"

"Not completely, but its coming. And that's really the reason I called you."

"That'll take some explaining."

"You know that drawing you circulated on your boy for that University killing?"

"Yeah."

"Well, I think I saw him."

Both detectives perked up at this and leaned forward.

"When?" asked Ron.

"Where?" Gene put in.

"I was over at the VA getting some therapy. For the knee. You ever been over there?"

"Couple times, why?" Ron asked.

"You know the Physical Therapy section?"

"Don't think so."

"Well, you know the cafeteria? And that outside area with tables?"

"Yeah, I know that area."

"The Physical Therapy area is on the other side of that eating area. Dark glass that allows good view of the eating area from inside."

"OK. Got it."

"So, yesterday I was on a stationary bike in PT as part of my daily routine. And I think I saw your guy doing a drug deal in the eating area."

"What? Tell me about it."

"Well, it looked like it anyway. He and one of the employees exchanged some small pieces of something. Did look a little funny 'cause I initially thought your guy was handing over money. You gotta understand, I'm suspicious of anyone exchanging items and especially when it looks like one of the items is money. That's kinda like my bread and butter."

Gene nodded and said, "Got it."

"Who was the employee?" Ron inquired.

"Couldn't see a name tag. Too far away. A white guy. About thirty or so. Thin. Short haircut. Maybe forty or might be a little younger."

"What exactly happened?"

"The whole thing took less than twenty seconds. They met, stuck out hands, exchanged stuff and parted. I was a little slow on the uptake and didn't even think there was anything going on until they were walking away from each other."

"Then?"

"I got off my bike and hustled out of PT into the eating area but they were both gone by then."

"You're sure that it was our guy?" Ron wanted to know.

"Pretty sure. Looked like your drawing and all. Right down to army jacket and dark baseball cap."

Gene and Ron exchanged a glance. Gene noted, "If that really was him, he has moved out of that apartment."

"Exactly what I was thinking, partner."

Harvey looked at each and asked, "Is this helpful?"

"Maybe so, Harv. Maybe so," Ron said shaking his head. "We thought we had a line on the guy's hidey-hole but he hasn't shown for several days and we were thinking maybe he was a runner. After the murder, you know. Now you see him apparently doing some business. We have to change our thinking about the apartment."

"Sorry, man. I know how it is to lose a thread, no matter how small."

"Right," Ron said standing up and giving his friend a fist-bump. As he started for the exit he turned back to ask, "What were you doing getting therapy at the VA?"

"That was the knee that got me 50 percent disabled when I left service. Injured in a jump in Bosnia."

"You were Airborne?"

"Yes sir. Proud part of the AA."

"Never understood the jumping out of perfectly good airplanes," Gene offered.

"Quickest way down," Harvey replied with big grin.

Chapter 24

"Ron, this is Tom. Your boy's name is Thomas Whelan."

"Great work, Tom, we might could get you a junior detective badge. You got social and address?"

"Of course I do. And that should be worth a senior detective badge."

"Maybe a whistle and a decoder ring."

Tom had done far more than the minimum in identifying Thomas Whelan. He had pulled the man's medical chart and discovered far more information about his care and living situation. Understanding that he was treading a fine line very close to stepping into violation of HIPAA, Tom curtailed the information he provided to Ron to include only the absolute necessary personal health information that pertained to the case.

Thomas Whelan was an active duty U. S. Army Ranger, recently injured in a special operation, details not included but an orthopedic surgeon like Tom Bolling could read between the lines. Whelan was mission bound and returned with significant injury to his left hip. He was treated acutely at his base and determined to need longer rehabilitation and subsequently placed on 90-day convalescent leave. The injury and the initial documented treatment were most consistent with secondary and tertiary blast injury. His home was a small town in western Kentucky, south of Cincinnati on route 42 and he had been referred to Cincinnati VA Medical Center for rehabilitation.

The VA physical therapist most savvy about hip injury and rehabilitation had been mobilized as part of his National Guard Unit and was on active duty so the VA referred Whelan to New City because of the renowned program there.

The initial evaluation of Whelan's hip injury showed a blown hip socket (the acetabulum) on the right which the radiologist thought was likely due to concussive force on his right side driving the femoral head into the joint. Surgeons in the Army both near the mission site and in Germany and those at the VA had concurred with a non-operative approach to remediation and rehabilitation. The most important reason for this decision rested with the patient's desire to return to his Ranger Team since a joint replacement would be disqualifying in and of itself.

Whelan had shown steady but slow improvement in therapy at New City in terms of strength and range of motion until four weeks ago. At that point his performance took a slight downturn and he became depressed. He visited with a psychologist but did not regain his previous positive attitude. And his physical progress demonstrably slowed.

On his latest visit to Physical Therapy, Whelan had shown he had the ability to perform at a moderately high level in all tests except running stairs two steps at a time. His scores were likely not sufficient for him to return to active duty as a Ranger. He had missed his last appointment with the therapist.

The local address he provided when he enrolled at the VAMC was the rental property Ron and Gene had identified. Tom conveyed a minimum of medical information to Ron but he did say that Whelan was an injured Army Ranger, improving in rehabilitation that had missed his last appointment.

CHAPTER 25

Gene finished reading the report that Tom had forwarded to them and leaned back in his chair. He looked across the desks at his partner. "Shall we re-examine our 'Knowns'?" he asked.

"Seems like the right time. Some things don't change but get clearer. We believe first, they were together earlier in the evening. We've got a video of them walking together from somewhere toward the University and now we think we have the address for that in the garage apartment at Garing's place. Second, we have the tape showing that he walked her back to campus and had coffee on the way."

Gene raised his hand to interrupt Ron.

"Point of order. We don't actually have any evidence that he walked her any closer to the University than to that coffee shop."

"I stand corrected. To restate, we have evidence that he walked her back toward the University at least as far as the coffee shop. And we have corroboration that he was with her when she had coffee shortly before her death."

"You mean the coffee shop owner's information?"

"Yes. That is exactly what I mean."

"Go on."

"Well, we kinda know that they left the coffee shop together."

"Not a proved fact, but I'll give you the inference."

"Three, he killed her in the little park."

"Objection, your honor. Attorney for the prosecution is assuming facts not in evidence."

"Damn it, Gene. I'm assuming that because they were together just a few blocks from where she was murdered less than 30 minutes later."

"I'm just saying, partner. Do you want to try to convince the judge of the accuracy of our case?"

"All right. Let me try Number Three again."

"The floor is all yours, counselor."

"Three, shortly after this couple left the coffee shop the young woman was killed on University grounds."

"Factual and acceptable to the defense."

Ron frowned at Gene in mock anger and said, "I think you are having too good a time with this."

"Just trying to insure we are really dealing with 'knowns', that's all. We don't want to have one of those denials from the judge when we ask for a warrant, do we."

Ron sighed and nodded. Gene was right. He went on without waiting for a signal.

"Four, according to our medical examiner, the cause of death was a 'neck snap' likely performed by a special operator."

"Five, Tom Whelan is a Ranger," Gene added, smiling at his partner across the desktops.

"Six, he seems to have taken a powder right after the murder." Ron was smiling again until Gene again held up his hand. "What now?"

"Well, did he really disappear and leave town?"

"OK, at least he seems to have abandoned the address we know. If he's the guy Harv saw yesterday at the VA, he's still around. You're right."

"We need to pick him up."

"I'll get out a BOLO." Ron pulled out a form and began writing the limited description they had of the man called "TJ."

CHAPTER 26

Ron pulled into his driveway and sat in the car for a few minutes before getting out. He had little reason to hurry into the house; Meg was not there and wouldn't be for several days. The day before they had been awakened by the call they had been expecting. Their daughter, Katie, was about to give birth to their first grandchild and the call was summoning her mother to be with her. Meg didn't delay; she was on the next plane out of Cincinnati.

Katie was a graduate of Ohio State with a degree in computer science. She met and later married a young assistant professor there teaching in the business school as part of his work on an MBA. Jonathan Olsson was a very nice young man, classic Swedish features and manners. Ron had some fun with him at first noting that his first name, Jon, seemed to be missing a letter but his last name, Olsson, had one too many.

The young couple was in Helena, Montana where the newly minted MBA found a teaching position at Carroll College. This small Catholic liberal arts school was planning on placing a greater emphasis on its Business programs and hired Jon to supplement the faculty in management and marketing. They had been in Montana for three years and it had taken Katie less than the first half of the first year to find a job that fit her, as well. She was quickly employed as a junior staffer in the office of the Speaker of the House in the Montana state legislature. Her job built on her computer skills and she quickly became a fixture in the Speaker's office by creating easily understood graphics of the Speaker's position on various topics.

When she became pregnant, Katie and Jon agreed to invite Meg for the delivery and the two women consulted daily on various aspects of pregnancy and labor. They finally agreed that, given the distance and roundabout way to get to Helena, Katie would call daily in the last two weeks before her due date and would otherwise notify her mother of any major event like her water breaking or onset of labor.

When she called the night before, she had seemed calm but the urgency in wanting her mother was clear. Meg tried to calm her down while Ron dug out the travel itinerary he had planned. Meg left later that morning and made it into Helena without difficulty that night. By which time any contractions Katie was feeling had abated. Her physician's exam revealed that she had not yet begun to advance toward delivery and had probably had something called Braxton-Hicks contractions.

Nonetheless Meg was now in Montana and the due date was within a week so she decided to stay. Everyone in Montana was apparently pleased with this decision. Ron was not. He was accepting of the idea of a mother helping her daughter through delivery but he didn't much care for the quiet and empty house that now faced him.

He went in the garage door and entered the kitchen. He saw on the breakfast table the newspaper right where he had left it, beside the dirty dishes. He had scrambled eggs and bacon for breakfast just to show his independence and the dishes were still there proudly proclaiming that no one was about to clean up. He looked in the refrigerator and found some devilled eggs and two pork chops. He heated up a skillet with some butter in the pan, sprinkled some salt and pepper on the chops and went looking for something to make a salad.

He found some slightly brown lettuce, half a green pepper and a bag of radishes and onions. All were quickly shredded and put in a large bowl and tossed around. When he put the chops into the hot skillet, he dressed the salad with some olive oil and white balsamic vinegar, like Meg had taught him. He salted and peppered and added some celery seed to the mix while tending to the chops.

The dinner was fine, good even. But not quite right because Meg wasn't there to ask about the day and to give him the latest on what was happening with Katie. Ron felt sad not to have that input and thought he should give Helena a call. Then he decided that sounded a little too needy. He would call tomorrow. Instead he grabbed a beer from the refrigerator and made himself rinse the dishes and put them all into the dishwasher, breakfast dishes, too.

Then he grabbed his beer and the newspaper and went into the living room, determined to work the daily crossword. He hadn't addressed a crossword puzzle since high school that he could remember, but how hard could it be?

Forty minutes later with only five words filled, Ron decided he was not ready for crossword puzzles and went upstairs to take a shower.

Chapter 27

"Walker. What are you doing over here in Narcotics?" This was a simple question from the Unit chief, Lieutenant Walter Matthews. The lieutenant, or 'L.T.' as his men referred to him, was a perfectly average guy in height, weight, hair and overall coloring, including his café-au-lait-colored skin. Some in the department thought these unremarkable characteristics were a major reason for Matthews' success in undercover operations and his rise to lead the unit.

Ron knew better. Walter Matthews was a shrewd and clever cop. He passed the lieutenant examination on his first try and his success in the field was due more to thorough planning and skillful execution than luck or appearance. Matthews and Ron had run a few cases together over the years and had respect for each other and their capabilities.

"Simple, Walt. I want to know why a BOLO I put out on a murder suspect got canned by someone over here."

"That was your BOLO? Sorry. I shoulda called. Come in and let me tell you what's happening over here." He turned toward his office and invited Ron to join him inside with a wave.

Ron was visibly upset by having his request for apprehending Tom Whelan squelched at all but having it done without his being notified of reasons behind such action was close to being a bridge too far. Even for a friend. "Why can't you tell me right here?"

"Oh. Well, I can. There really shouldn't be a secret. I'm sorry we didn't come to you right away."

"We've lost a day with a probable killer wandering the streets."

"Again. I apologize. We were scrambling around and I didn't think to get someone to back up the blockade. C'mon in the office. You should be sitting down, anyway."

Ron sat in one of the industrial metal chairs that were scattered throughout the building. He sat straight up not touching the back of the chair and watched Walter Matthews' every move.

Walt sat in his own chair behind the desk and said, "Are you aware of the increase in opioid deaths in the city?"

"I'm aware the number is up and they aren't being referred to Homicide."

"There's a reason for that. These deaths are considered 'accidental' and weren't even being reported to us in the Police Department as suspicious."

"Why not?"

"Are you familiar with the legal use of narcotics in this country?"

"Somewhat, I guess. You mean prescription pain-killers, right?"

"Yes, I do. We have had a problem in this country for more than a century with narcotics and have bumbled our way around legislation until we have created a double-headed monster."

"Explain that to me. You aren't involved in enforcing oversteps in the legal market, are you?"

"Technically, no. Remember this national problem began when patent medicines were the rage right after the Civil War. Most likely got into the national consciousness because of the number of war wounded. But the traveling salesmen pushed the drugs for a wide variety of ailments, successfully by the way, since the drugs made everybody get 'high' and generally feel better for a while."

"You're talking a hundred-plus years ago, Walt."

"I am. But that's partly where the national taste and habit began. And it was about 80 years ago that things developed to divide the users into two separate groups. Laws were passed to limit the sale of these drugs to those prescribed by licensed physicians. That decision was not based on limiting the drugs because they were effective but because they were addictive."

"And the resulting two groups of users were . . .?"

"Legal users and illegal users."

"And that's been your focus, then, the illegal users?"

"Right. For a while it was clear what the demarcation was. Legal users had a prescription and got their drugs from a pharmacist in a well-lit store during the daytime. On the other hand, the illegal users were buying their drugs from shady guys in a back alley, usually at night."

"So, you ended up with an important job."

"Well, things started getting muddy 20-30 years ago."

"That's still before you took this job."

"Yeah, but its important to know how we got here."

"All right. Go on. I'm sure you have a point."

"Oh, I do. I just want you to understand it. At some point back in the 90s medical writings began to emphasize that doctors weren't treating pain effectively. Apparently some studies showed that even hospitalized patients had significant pain."

"What's that got to do with anything, Walt?"

"Stick with me, brother. Those studies suggested that doctors were afraid of the addicting nature of narcotics and were underusing them. So, a big emphasis developed in the legal market to use more narcotics. OxyContin gave the doctors a way to do that and a lot of unused narcotics started showing up in people's medicine cabinets."

"And taken by their kids and put on the street." Ron suddenly saw the big picture Walt was painting. "But there are big campaigns now to limit the use of narcotics. I remember when Meg had our kids the doctors were very tight with the drugs."

"Pendulum. By that time they were back to undertreating. Sending people home with few pills and rarely highly effective ones. More often the low dose codeine."

"I still am having trouble seeing the value of this history lesson. I watched '*Drugsick*.'"

"Well, think of it this way: over the last two generations, Americans have come to think of drug-users as either legitimate or illegal. The legitimate ones have a prescription and the others lurk around in dark alleys and are frequently homeless street people. So, when one of the latter shows up in an Emergency Room somewhere everyone assumes their plight is due to their illicit behavior. Their presence and treatment becomes of interest to the police and their case is recorded as 'overdose'."

"Yeah. I see that."

""But if a 'legal user' shows up in the Emergency Room somewhere with clear overdose, and I mean they have an obvious response to Narcan and family says they have a prescription, then they are handled as a victim and the incident is not reported to police."

"Because they are in possession of a prescription narcotic?"

"And because they are considered a 'legal user' who probably got 'a little too much'. So they get sympathy and are never brought to our attention."

"But something must have changed recently. You are telling me about deaths you're calling 'suspicious'. That doesn't sound particularly like ones in the illegal cohort. So, who are these suspicious cases?"

"Let me give you some statistics. Deaths in the city from provable opioid overdose are nearly twice what they were last year."

"OK. That's impressive," Ron was less perturbed with his friend hearing the magnitude of the problem he was dealing with.

"And the population being hit the worst appears to be a brand new one. Elderly people in their home. We're not talking about druggies on the street or wild teenagers. These are settled, sometimes retired people, living the quiet life. Almost all of them had a prescription and were considered just unlucky. Not illegal."

"How did you find out about this, then. Sounds like they weren't reported."

"Not officially. No, we got our information through a backdoor channel. You know Henry Yang?"

"Only by face to nod at."

"Henry's daughter-in-law is a nurse in a local Emergency Room. She mentioned to him that they had seen several of these patients in the last few months and Henry did some digging. It's true and this increase is worrisome because it was going on under our radar."

"How are they getting the drugs?" Ron asked. "Are they going out at night or is this a home-delivery service?"

"We don't know. Some of them are single individuals with some kind of home companion during the day. Others involve one of a couple and the other one says they are not doing anything illegal."

"What's that got to do with my BOLO?"

"Harvey told me about your guy at the VA. We think he's mixed in with this new wave in some way."

"On what grounds?"

"We've got an informant in the local distribution racket. He's been giving us information for about two years. He says there's new muscle in town and your boy is one of them."

"So?"

"Scooter says this new bunch hung around and watched their delivery on the streets but then kinda melted away. The locals had been expecting a turf was but these new guys don't seem to have any turf."

"And? Did you check some of the Senior Centers?"

"Our informant also says there's something big going down tonight. A major meeting for distributors or something like that. We couldn't take the chance on your picking him up and giving away our chance to catch the big guys."

"What's your reason for thinking the 'big guys' are involved in this action tonight?"

"The informant says your guy is called 'T.J.' and he's one of the two major lieutenants for a new boss in town. Apparently he's been seen around town dressed like a army veteran and at other times in a suit and tie."

"Maybe visiting your elderly victims."

"Not that we can tell. Anyway, he is supposed to be at the meet tonight and we were afraid if he got nabbed, the meet might get pushed off."

"OK. I can understand all that. Still would have appreciated a call."

"Completely my bad. Still friends?"

Slow nod from Ron and a handshake between the men followed.

"Do you want any additional hands on board tonight?" Ron asked as he exited the office. "Gene and I would go home early if not."

"We don't know where this meeting is supposed to take place but if its wide open I would certainly want some help on the perimeter."

"Don't worry about us trying to get the glory. We're happiest when we can say, 'Stop. Police.' and they do."

"I'll call you in a couple of hours, OK?"

"In the meantime, I'd like to talk to your CI."

"What for?"

"More information about my murder suspect. I need to know more about him than a nickname."

CHAPTER 28

Ron walked into the break room and sat next to "Scooter" Parsens, the confidential informant for Walt. Parsens was only thirty years old according to his jacket but he looked closer to fifty. His thin, pock-marked and pasty face was framed by unkempt, dirty brown hair. His eyes flickered around the room, not really settling on anything in particular as if he had a nervous system disease. Parsens was hunched over a vending machine sandwich and a soda can, warily eying any movement in the room or the hallway outside. His arms rested on the table protecting his food and drink.

"Scooter?" Walt said as he walked into the room behind Ron. "This is Detective Looney. He wants to talk to you about T.J."

"Looney? That's crazy man, Looney."

"You can call me Walker," Ron said sitting down and leaning away from the obviously nervous individual to lessen any perception of threat.

"Looney Walker, OK."

"Can I ask you about 'TJ'?"

"Hmmm." His mouth was full and he barely nodded

"You've seen this T.J. person?"

He swallowed and took a gulp of his soda. "Oh yeah. Seen him more'n I want." Parsens spoke quietly with his head down.

"What does the 'T.J.' stand for? What's his name?" Ron probed.

"I don' know, man. He's T.J. That's all."

"What can you tell me about him?"

"Tough. He's tough. And mean." This admission came only after a moment of what passed for reflection by Scooter.

"How do you know that?"

"Seen him hit guys for nothing. Me, too. Don't wanna be around him at all."

"Is this what he looks like?" Ron put the police artist drawings on the table in front of Scooter.

Scooter took his time looking at the drawing before answering, "Yeah, pretty much. Ain't' got no beard though."

"What else can you tell me about him? His voice, his accent, how he walks." Ron spoke plainly, without any pressure on Scooter.

Scooter was quiet and took another bite of his sandwich and began chewing slowly. For a brief moment Ron thought he was ignoring the question he had been asked. Then Scooter nodded and swallowed and said, "He spits a lot. And he walks funny."

"How's that? Ron had his notebook and pen out to write the description

"What?"

"How does he walk funny?" "He's got some kinda limp. And he don't like it when anybody notices. He hit one guy for suggesting that he couldn't run. Hurt him, too."

Ron looked at Scooter solemnly before asking, "Does he carry a weapon?"

"Uh huh," came the answer through the last of the sandwich. "He's got a pistol and a knife. Pistol in his back pocket and a knife in his ankle strap."

Ron wrote these details in his book.

"Do you know where he stays?"

"Whatta ya mean?" Scooter scratched his head.

"I mean, where could we find him? Where does he sleep?"

"I dunno. He's just around sometimes."

"How is he dressed when he's around?"

" Sometimes in a suit but mostly in that army jacket and ball cap."

"What does he do when he is wearing a suit?" Ron leaned forward too far as he asked this and Scooter pulled back. "I dunno. Goes off somewhere."

"Is he going to be at this meeting tonight?"

"Probably. The Boss is going to be there and he's usually got T.J. and Pokemon around him."

"Who's Pokemon?" Ron looked at Walt.

"We know about this guy," Walt said. "Another new guy in town and part of the muscle brought in by this 'Boss'."

"Are T.J. and Pokemon always together?" Ron asked Scooter.

"Nah. T.J. comes around a lot by hisself. We never see Pokemon without him being with the Boss."

"OK, Scooter. Thanks for that information." Ron stood to leave the room.

"That's good, huh? Can I get another sandwich?"

CHAPTER 29

Gene listened carefully to Ron's explanation of the BOLO cancellation and Walt Matthews' story about the opioid deaths.

"Does this add anything to our list of 'Knowns'?"

"Possibly. If the Narcs are right about this being our guy, then we can add 'drug dealer' to the list."

"I don't see that adding any weight to our case."

"Probably not. Not any evidence we found of drug use by Margaret, at least." Ron agreed as he leaned back in his chair.

"Still want to talk to him as the major suspect. Compare him to the video, get the coffee shop owner to look at him, all that stuff," Gene leaned forward to emphasize the steps he still saw as necessary.

"Interested enough to join the Narcs on their operation tonight?"

"Will they promise to either run our guy straight to us or make sure he doesn't get hurt?"

"These guys aren't big on promises. You know that." Ron came forward in his chair to emphasize his point.

"I know they're not big on keeping them."

"Well, we know they're down at least one guy with Harv on rehab assignment. I think I'll go if Walt calls and asks for help."

"Alright. I will, too, then," Gene said rising from his chair and snagging his jacket. "But I'm going home to change. Call if you hear from him."

"You got it." Ron watched his partner grab his jacket and leave before turning to look at the paperwork on his desk. The Murder Book he and Gene were assembling was comfortably full, but Ron knew it contained mostly negative findings: nothing from interviews on campus, nothing from all the door knocking except the garage apartment, but nothing useful from Garing about the renter, nothing about habits, not even a good picture. Against all that the scant information they could count as 'Known' was pretty slim and without a good deal more that information would not support an arrest or murder charge.

He leaned back in his chair and thought, 'May be our best chance at getting this guy is to participate in the operation tonight. But that's not likely to make our case anyway.'

A few minutes later, after fiddling with some items on his desk, Ron got up and took his partner's advice. He left the office and went home to change.

CHAPTER 30

He was at home when he got the call. Walt's informant indicated the meeting that night was to be held at a storage facility west of the river. The area backed up to a residential area and Walt realized he would need some additional bodies to post the area. Ron took the information and called Gene with specifics about where the police would be gathering.

Ron had changed into jeans, running shoes and a dark blue hooded sweater. He clipped his weapon on his belt and made sure he had two spare magazines before leaving. At the rendezvous site he paired up with Gene and they were given instructions about where they were to take up an observation post. Walt had obtained a Google Earth photo of the storage facility and surrounding area and used that to place his teams.

Walt wanted Ron and Gene in the residential cul-de-sac about a block from the rear of the storage facility. They would remain in the car unless there was trouble and one or more of the gang tried to flee in their direction. As the briefing progressed Ron noted the presence of a high chain-link fence at the rear of the storage facility that should prevent any flight in the direction of their post. He and Gene were placed where they would be unlikely to come in contact with any of the players.

Ron drove and the detectives took up their position shortly before dark. All the way to their post Gene had complained that they should have obtained a larger car for several reasons.

"You know we can't get out and walk around, right?"

"I know that very well, Gene."

"Well, this tiny little leg room here is gonna be problem for me."

"Move the seat back."

"Its back as far as it will go."

"Buck up, soldier. This is likely to be a long night. Let's not start with a hard pucker."

"And you never did get the springs on this seat fixed, did you?"

"The springs are not broken."

"Well, they sure don't work. Look at this," he said starting to bounce up and down.

"Stop that. We're going to sit quietly and that's that."

"Next time I'm bringing my car."

"Uh huh."

Once parked in a location that allowed visual access to the storage facility through the front window, they settled in. Neither man smoked, so cigarette glow was not a problem. Unlike younger officers they were trained so sit and watch without having to check their phone every few minutes. Prying eyes would have thought the car was empty.

Each man had brought a small thermos of coffee but they did not intend to start on food or drink early in the watch; the last thing they wanted was a bladder call at some critical moment later.

"Did you sweep the area with the NVG?" Ron asked. They had been provided only one pair of night vision goggles.

"Yeah. No movement. And it's not really dark yet."

"What's that big shadow at this end of the right side units?"

The storage facility was composed of two parallel buildings of multiple units each facing the other building. The area fenced by the chain link was several feet away from the end of the two buildings. The only entrance into the fenced facility was the driveway from a local street at the far end from where Ron and Gene were positioned.

At the rendezvous Ron had asked Walt what he thought about the wisdom of the drug dealers having a meeting where they could be trapped in a blind alley. That didn't seem right to him but Walt had shaken the question off saying, "I guess they're feeling pretty secure. We haven't taken any of them down since they've been here."

Everyone had studied the aerial photograph of the area before leaving the rendezvous and Ron didn't remember seeing any large structure at the far end of the units from the entrance.

"What is that thing?" he asked again.

"Looks like another building of some kind. Big, square and long."

"That wasn't on the photo."

Gene agreed, shifting in his seat, "Yeah, but Walt said those pictures were a month or more old."

"So it's new. Could have something to do with these drug guys. We better watch that shadow carefully. We'll be able to see over there better when it gets a little darker."

CHAPTER 31

The night did get darker, the waning moon not providing illumination and the orange lights around the storage area seemed unable to penetrate the darkness. Gene and Ron took half-hour rotations with the NVG apparatus, carefully scanning the end of the facility. Their parking place was more than a city block away from the facility and the area between was a poorly maintained field previously zoned residential. They were parked at the end of the cul-de-sac where some hopeful developer had cut some driveways into the field where houses should have been built but never were.

"When was the last time you did one of these stakeouts?" Gene asked as he dug in his knapsack for some food. "Been years. Never did take to it much. I prefer moving. And don't think you're gonna eat those crackers in my car."

"Man, I'm hungry. We've been out here way past my bedtime snack."

"I don't want cracker crumbs all over the seats."

"I'll eat over my knapsack."

"Don't get crumbs in the car."

"OK. OK."

The next time Gene had the night vision apparatus, Ron reached into the back and pulled up a small bottle of water. Gene immediately countered, "So, it's alright if you imbibe but not OK for me to eat some peanut butter."

"I'm just having a sip of water and I'm not crumbling it on the seat."

"I'm just saying, the rules seem different."

"Can you see any of Walt's guys?" Ron inquired, trying to keep the conversation more on the task at hand and less on the perceived shortcomings of his automobile or his rules about food.

"Nope. They've gone to ground."

They sat in silence for a while. Then Ron picked up the NVG apparatus and scanned the area near the storage area. Almost immediately he noticed a movement across the field, near the fence. At first it appeared to be some breeze causing some of the taller weeds to wave about but then he caught a brief glimpse of a darker shadow close to the ground. As he watched, the shadow seemed to disappear at the fence line. Ron continued scanning the area for a few more seconds, and then asked Gene, "Did you ever see any of the tall grass out there moving?"

"You mean like someone was crawling through?"

"Yeah."

"Don't think so. You see something?"

Ron sat upright in his seat, leaning forward toward the dashboard. "And there's another one. Look, just to the right of the big thing at the end," he commented as he handed the glasses to Gene.

"Don't really see anything. . . . Hold it! Yeah, a dark blob. Looked like it was right by the fence and then it disappeared. Looked a little like it went through the fence." Gene handed Ron the glasses.

He scanned the area briefly before saying, "That's two and maybe we missed some others. Better tell Walt. Not only are there more in there than he thinks but there's a back door out. If those guys start coming out this way we don't have the numbers to catch them."

Ron handed the glasses back to Gene and picked up the radio Walt had given them.

"Team Leader, this is Harry One, over."

Silence on the radio.

"Team Leader, this is Harry One, over."

Silence persisted on the radio.

"Team Leader, this is Harry One, are you there?" Ron's voice was not any louder but was more demanding.

Pause.

"Team Leader, this is Harry One, do you read."

Gene put down the glasses and turned to Ron, "Are you kidding me?"

Ron dropped the radio on the console and pulled out his cell phone. He dialed Metro Central and asked for the narcotics command post. A minute later he was talking to Walt's deputy back at the police headquarters.

"Where's Walt? He's not answering his radio."

"Walt turned his radio off. He thinks there's too much chance the guys they're after might hear them and get scared off."

"Well, he's left us out here in the boonies with absolutely no communication!"

"The whole team is on comms." The deputy indicated that the narcotics team members were each wearing earpieces with close quarters communication. His inflection indicated he thought that was an appropriate move and that Ron should understand.

"Well, he didn't include us in that. Look, we've seen some guys slipping in the back way through the fence and Walt needs to know there's more people in there than he knows."

The Deputy responded, "I can text him that info."

"Do it. That also means there's a back door he doesn't have covered."

Almost at the very moment he disconnected his phone, Ron saw flashes of light between the storage buildings and heard the sound of gunfire. The brief volley was followed by darkness and quiet for about six seconds before another quick set of flashes and sounds of another volley. Then, as he and Gene watched, alternating the NVG between them, dark figures ran between the buildings and seemed to be heading directly for them or more correctly toward the fence at the rear of the facility.

As the figures approached the fence they disappeared and then reappeared and started moving to the right or the left, alternating as they came out of the storage area.

"They got out of the facility," Gene said. "And they're scattering."

Ron made one last attempt to reach Walt on the radio. "Team Leader, this is Harry One, several bogies left through the rear fence. We are pursuing toward the river."

He started the car, backed out of the driveway and spun around, not turning on his lights. Then, tires screeching, he shot down the street toward the entrance into the cul-de-sac.

CHAPTER 32

R on raced down the residential street toward the cross street, weaving slightly to avoid the cars parked on either side. Gene was rummaging in the equipment bag at his feet trying to locate their powerful lanterns. Ron felt like it was taking them far too long to get to the end of the street and tried to increase his speed when suddenly he saw the stop sign almost hidden from view by a parked truck.

He slammed on his brakes and skidded halfway into the intersection before he was able to turn right and accelerate. Tires screeching on the pavement he began searching for the next street into the area behind the storage facility. "Gene, can you see the street sign?," he bellowed.

Gene had been tossed wildly about on the raceway turn and just settled into his seat, "Just ahead."

"Got it," Ron said as he downshifted and threw the car through the intersection and sped down the street parallel to where he began. There was nothing subtle about their approach to the open field as the engine of Ron's car was racing and his headlights were weaving and bobbing with the unevenness of the street. As he reached the end of the new cul-de-sac he slammed the car into park and he and Gene jumped out with weapons drawn.

"Catch," Gene said as he sailed a torch over the hood to Ron. They immediately headed off in different directions looking for movement in the grass of the field. They wove the light beams from their torches over a field in front of themselves and crossing over into the area covered by the other.

Neither man spoke or called out as they covered the area watching and listening for any sound that might help them locate the men who had fled the storage facility. About ten minutes after they began their sweep of the area, Ron saw lights and figures coming through the fence. Walt's men had cleared the facility and had joined the search in the field.

At Ron's signal, Gene joined him to turn back into the neighborhood. Ron noted, "If they weren't in front of us, they had to have gotten behind us. How long did it take to get over here?"

"Probably two minutes, maybe a little more."

"Time enough to run across that field?"

"Probably. The distance from the storage area to the neighborhood is barely a block. Anyone in decent shape could make that. Especially if they knew the terrain and if they knew where they were going." Gene was measuring the distance with his torch light.

"So, they likely got into the neighborhood and between these houses."

"How many came this way?"

"I saw two before I handed you the glasses."

"I think I saw the same ones."

"So, two guys on foot in the area. Possibly armed. I'll tell Walt."

They took up position with their back to the storage area, facing into the quiet and dark neighborhood. The open field area crossed another unused gravel road and merged into the rear yards of houses for the next two blocks. There were no lights in the backyards and the tree growth made it impossible to gain a skyline to help with detecting movement. They let their light play across the roadway and through the area but they saw no further indication of the runners.

Moments later Ron and Walt made contact on the radio and Walt responded by calling for a five-block perimeter around the area. Time crept on and the number of torch lights in the neighborhood increased but without any sign of the individuals they were seeking. Houses remained dark and some of the officers ran through the rear yards without using their lights to cover a lot of ground. One officer ran into a wire fence around a rear yard and flipped over into the yard, landing on his back. That event caused others to move more slowly and by the time they had covered two blocks searching the rear yards, almost twenty minutes had passed since Ron had talked with Walt.

Small groups of officers exited the rear yard area at various points somewhat short of a block apart and stopped to assess. They remained there, watching the street for activity for another thirty minutes until Walt radioed everyone to call off the search. He indicated he was going back to the storage area and wanted everyone else to be in the office for a meeting at eight o'clock meeting back at headquarters to review the action.

Members of the Drug Unit began slowly walking back to the front of the storage area where they would be picked up by patrols. Gene sidled up to Ron and said, "Well, at least our car is right here. I think we got time to grab a breakfast sandwich before the meeting, don't you?"

CHAPTER 33

W alt's meeting at headquarters was raucous. Usually at eight o'clock in the morning every unit was rather quiet as men and women came to work somberly and with automated movements. Normally, it would take a major intervention in the room to get everyone talking and even then there needed to have been time for the second cup of coffee. But this morning was different. Each officer present had something to say and it appeared not to require that anyone be listening. In fact, if the speaker thought he was being ignored there was a tendency to just speak more loudly. Conversations toward the rear of the room continued after Walt stood up in front and started speaking. He had to call for quiet twice before he got enough reduction in noise to be heard.

Ron noted that for a leader whose high profile mission had blown up in his face, Walt seemed relatively unperturbed; not calm but almost grinning at times.

"All right. Things didn't go just exactly the way we planned out there tonight." Walt said this twice to get everyone's attention and to bring some sobriety to the room. "I'm not completely sure why but one reason is we didn't know about the hole in the fence. Did anybody go out there and do surveillance?"

There was silence for almost a minute while the men of Narco looked around at each other. Finally a voice from the back spoke up, "We thought you didn't want any activity that would spook the gang."

"Well, yes I guess I did say that," Walt admitted. "Still, somebody could've checked." More silence. No one wanted to say the obvious, if the leader wanted that checked he should have made it an assignment.

"All right. I was even warned that the dead end seemed unrealistic. I should've thought they might have cut the fence. That was why we put the Homicide guys back there. I mean, just in case."

Ron spoke up, "We didn't pick up anyone coming in that way 'til the last minute anyway. And when they ran to the right and the left coming out we had to make a choice."

"How long did you take to get over to the other street?"

"Gene thought it was two minutes or so."

"They couldn't have gotten far in that time," said one of the Narco officers.

"Enough to get into the neighborhood. All those dark back yards, places to hide," replied the guy next to him.

"Our five block perimeter should've pinned them in, though."

Ron spoke up again. "I think it probably did pin them in. They had a house to go to in that neighborhood. Maybe more than one. That's why they split up." Walt looked at Ron questioningly. He went on, "They probably have a hidey-hole in that neighborhood. Somewhere they can get in and out of without being noticed. The hole in the back gate became their entrance to the storage area. No messing with the entrance and all those vapor light."

"Yeah, we didn't see anybody come in the front gate," another officer offered. "They must've all come in the back way."

"So, everybody got in through that back fence?"

"Appears so."

"What started the gunfire?" Gene wanted to know

One of the Narco men spoke up, "That was me. We hadn't seen anybody come in and I was moving my position to get closer to the back end of the facility and one of them must've seen me."

"So, that was them shooting?" asked Harvey.

"To start with. I shot twice at gun flashes but when they started moving to the fence we couldn't shoot because of the neighborhood right behind them," the man answered

"Was this a set-up?" asked a voice from the rear of the room.

"I don't think so." Walt shook his head. "If it was I think they'd have put up more of a fight. Plus, I'm pretty sure they wouldn't have taken us to this place on a set-up." He seemed very certain of this and his attitude made everyone pause.

Gene asked, "Why do you say that?"

"Well, after we stopped pursuit four of us went back to see if we could figure out why the meeting was going to be at that facility. Turns out one of the gang got there early and had unlocked one of the three padlocks on that big transport storage container."

"So, that is something new?"

"Oh, yeah. And it's a jackpot." Suddenly the suppressed smile on the face of Walt Matthews broke out in a huge grin. "Tell 'em, Jim," he motioned to his assistant who had been quiet until this point.

Jim stood and the room fell silent. "We opened the transport container and inside was this!" He clicked a remote and a projector turned on and lit up a slide of the inside of the transport. The picture showed a small-wheeled vehicle inside the transport, the vehicle was shaped as an elongated cuboid and appeared to have a set of double doors at the rear.

"What's that?" was asked by several voices.

"That, gentlemen is the missing robovan. This automated delivery vehicle was being used to transport a shipment of fentanyl from a distributor here in town to a warehouse. The vehicle is programmed to take surface roads, trigger automated garage doors and park itself in the warehouse."

Several voices came at once. "Driver-less?" "Fentanyl" "How's it work?"

Walt held up his hand to call for quiet again. "Look," he said, "we've only had this information for an hour or so. I don't know the answer to all your questions right now. Jim has more to tell you."

"The van was unlocked and inside we found not only the fentanyl but also boxes with packets of $100 dollar bills. We estimate we picked up between 600 and 700,000 dollars in addition to grabbing their entire drug supply."

The room erupted in shouts and applause. What had seemed to be a busted operation had turned out to be one of the biggest bonanzas in the history of the Drug Unit.

CHAPTER 34

Later, Ron and Gene sat in the small coffee shop to discuss the impact of the night's activities on their search for a murder suspect.

"We didn't see anybody well enough to identify them," Gene said. "Therefore, we don't know if our Tom guy was there or not."

"Doesn't matter. We didn't get him, either way."

Gen shook his head and took a bite of his breakfast sandwich.

Ron went on, "How long have we been on his crib, now? More'n three days without a sign. With the big whiff last night on catching anybody, I bet they'll all be rabbiting out of here by the end of the day."

"Why would he run now if he didn't run after committing a murder?"

"I'm assuming the information from Scooter was correct and that T.J. Tom is wrapped up in this drug deal in some way. The evidence is they have been making a killing at it - and that's no pun intended."

"Yeah, I agree. Close to three-quarters of a mil. That's a killing, alright," Gene mumbled through a large bit of the sandwich.

"So, until last night this Tom had a strong incentive to stay in the area. We certainly weren't nipping at his heels for the murder. He had no reason to feel pressed about getting out of town when there's a pot full of money to be made."

"And now?" "I'm guessing he and all the gang are going to have to cut their losses and leave. They've lost their stash and they've lost their cash."

"That's kinda funny, Ron."

"I was being serious. Poetry just comes out at times. They lost all or most of the money they made here and they no longer have the drugs to sell, so what's to hold them around?"

"Probably nothing. I agree," Gene finished his sandwich and brushed his crumbs off the table. "Have you got a plan for going after this Whelan guy?

"Not much of one, I must admit. But there may be something in the apartment that would give us an idea about where to start looking again."

"Like what? He abandoned that place."

"Maybe he did so because we found it and he didn't have time to clean it out. We've had eyes on since we first talked to Garing, and if he spotted us, he hasn't had a chance to come back and clean up."

"Well, let's go hit the place before lunch," Gene said getting up from the table.

"You really are something, aren't you, partner?" Ron shook his head. "You barely got through that breakfast sandwich and you're already planning lunch."

"Listen, man. In this business you've got to take the long view and plan ahead. If I left it up to my partner as to when we would stop and eat, I'd probably have to go on intravenous feedings."

"Yeah, well, your partner is gonna go see if Scooter can give us more information. You can go clean out the apartment."

CHAPTER 35

R on walked into the Drug Unit carrying a cup of coffee. He found Harvey Upton at the copy machine near the center of the area. "Harv, I'd like to have another talk with Scooter."

"Hey, Ron. That's OK by me. I don't know where he is. Let me finish this and I'll find out."

Taking his copies, Harvey retraced his steps to his desk and sat down, indicating to Ron to have a seat next to his. He picked up the phone and dialed. "Walt? Walker's here to see Scooter. Do you know if he's still here?"

Getting a short response, Harvey turned to Ron and said, "Walt thinks he cut out earlier. Wanted to get out while everybody was at the meeting so no one would spot him at the station."

Ron bowed his head for a second, then asked, "Any idea where he hangs?"

"Look, I don't think you should be out looking for him right now. We have some other feedback that this gang thinks somebody leaked about the meeting."

"What if I arrested him, say for vagrancy?"

"They're on to that stuff. Likely any attention will be bad for him."

"Listen, Harv, I think he's got some more information he can tell me about this guy and I really want to talk with him. I have good information his name really is Tom Whelan."

"Where'd you get that information?"

"Contact in the veteran community. He's a Ranger and deadly. We need to get him off the street - now!"

"Ron, you need to cool it right now, OK? Scooter is our only real lead into this gang and we don't want anything to happen to him."

"I understand about your CI and all that. If you do talk with him, can I get in some questions, too?" Ron leaned forward earnestly.

"I suppose. If he's in here, sure. I'm not certain we can do that if he calls in."

"I really want to talk with him."

"I hear you, brother. I hear you."

CHAPTER 36

R on was sitting at his desk in the Dick Pen, waiting for Jim-Bob to finish copying some materials so he could get to the copier. Ron kept flipping through the pages of the Murder Book and wondering if the pages were all in the right order. At least once in the recent past, the clue to solving an intricate murder plot had involved putting events in a different order than they were discovered. But, as he looked through the pages he noted these events were already arranged by chronology. No easy solution this time. He toyed with his brief report on the drug raid wondering if it even belonged in the file on Margaret's murder.

Reviewing events and facts in his mind, Ron created a simple timeline from the list of facts he now knew from several sources. First, "TJ" has been in the city for several weeks. He rented an apartment. He was dealing drugs on the VA campus. His real name was Tom Whelan. He was a Ranger, a special operator with skill to kill with a neck snap. He had apparently been seeing Margaret for a couple of weeks. He was injured and not likely going back to active duty as an operator so he was probably looking for some way to make money once he got out of the service. Drugs came to the fore possibly because he used them and may have had contact to get in with the ring dealing drugs around Cincinnati.

Ron corrected himself about a couple of those things on his list. Not all of those things were 'knowns'. The drug connection was not yet proved but what Harvey Upton had told him certainly made that connection make sense. And, there's all that stuff that 'Scooter' had said: TJ was a main man in the drug ring. He was mean and carried both a pistol and a knife. He had a limp and he spit often. If he was to take what Scooter said as fact, then the drug connection was not just circumstantial.

Jim-Bob left the copy machine and Ron got up to go there for his copies of the drug raid report. As he returned to his desk he took a peek at the coffee pot. It appeared to be about one-third full of a murky fluid that Ron thought might contain particulate matter. He decided that he would try the coffee shop down the street while waiting for a call back from Walt about Scooter.

Feeling slightly better about the case than he had earlier, Ron stopped off at Thor's office and asked if he could bring a cup back for the captain. For the briefest of instances, Ron thought he was about to get 'the Look' but Captain Thorason smiled and nodded agreement.

Ron realized it was almost noon when he got to the coffee shop and had to stand in line to order. He decided to get something to eat as well while he worked his way to the front and got a ham and cheese sandwich as well as coffee. He decided to take his order back to work since most of the seating area was taken and he wanted the captain to have hot coffee. So, he was mounting the stairs when his mobile phone rang and he had no hands to handle the call.

He sat the coffees on the stairs and answered, "Walker."

"Hey, buddy, It's Walt."

"Thanks for calling back."

"This is the first chance I've had to return the call."

"I know. Big hero has lots of news interviews. Probably up for Key to the City, right?"

"That's not what took so long." Walt's voice was not light-hearted and Ron began to suspect things had gone wrong for him.

"What's the problem, Walt?"

"We found Scooter."

"I don't like the way that sounds."

"It sounds exactly the way it is. We found him downtown. In an alley. Shot in the back of the head."

"Crap. I wanted to get him to tell me more about Whelan."

"Well, He won't be telling anything anymore. Executed by those bastards."

"I don't suppose there's anything to tie my guy to the drug guys?"

"Not at the moment. We're out interviewing some on the streets but I don't expect we will hear anything. The 'protests' were all over that area and nobody saw anything. It's like they were wearing blindfolds instead of masks."

"You got any other eyes into this organization?" Ron asked, feeling that his only chance to learn about the mysterious Tom Whelan had vanished.

"Not now. I'll call if I do."

Ron put his phone back in his pocket, picked up the coffees and headed back up the stairs to the office. Thor was on the phone and simply waved 'thanks' so Ron went to his desk and ate his ham and cheese. All he could think was, "I hope Gene has better luck than I did."

Chapter 37

G ene took two other officers with him when he went to visit Garing's garage apartment. One of them was a crime scene expert whose job was to collect trace evidence and check fingerprints in the apartment. Gene chose to use a department car from the pool but not a black and white. He drove and thought the driver's seat was definitely better than the shotgun seat in Ron's car.

Garing was sitting on his front porch when they arrived and Gene got out and went up the sidewalk to talk to him before the other officers left the car.

"Good morning, Mr. Garing. I'm Detective Novalchek, we met the other day."

"I remember," the elderly man said not moving from his chair. He rubbed his eyes and picked up a cup of coffee from a small table and took a swallow.

"Mr. Garing, we would like to look inside the apartment today. I've brought two other officers to assist me."

"I can see that."

"We have a warrant to examine the apartment. Do you have a key?"

"Course I do. I own that 'partment." Garing remained seated, not making any movement other than to drink from his coffee cup.

"Would you mind getting that key for us, sir?" Gene asked, beginning to have some concern about Garing's likelihood of cooperation.

"Sure. Sure," Garing said and he started to get out of the chair by leaning forward. Gene watched as the man leaned almost too far and then sat back in the chair with an effort. Then he tried leaning forward again but still did not succeed in getting to his feet.

Gene wondered what this pretense was all about and he went up the stairs to help Garing to his feet. As he approached the chair, Garing waved his arms about and again tried to lean himself into an upright position. This time he did go too far and would have fallen forward if Gene had not caught him.

Gene grabbed the frail old man by his arm and spun him around to help him stand. Facing each other, Gene was acutely aware of the smell of alcohol on Garing and noticed the redness of the man's eyes. He helped Garing back down into the chair and said, "Perhaps you could just tell me where the key is, Mr. Garing?"

"Yeah, that's good," he said reaching for the coffee cup. Gene intercepted the cup and smelled the bourbon in it. Without any coffee.

"Is your door locked, here, sir?"

"No. No reason. Nobody around."

"Where do you keep the key to the apartment, sir? Can we go in your house to get it?"

"Sure, sure. Right by the door. See?"

Gene signaled to the uniformed officer who then opened the front door and entered the house. Gene moved the cup out of Garing's reach by setting it on the floor of the porch behind his chair. The uniformed officer appeared in the doorway holding a set of keys on a large ring that held several smaller rings with several tabs on various keys.

Gene took the keys and showed them to Garing. "Are these your keys, sir?"

"Yes. You bet," he said with semi-vigorous nodding of his head.

"Which key opens the apartment?

"Lemme see." Garing fumbled around with the set of keys and finally held up one. "The Yale one. Only Yale I got."

"Alright, Mr. Garing. We're going to go look around in the apartment. Will you be all right here on the porch?"

"What? Sure. I sit here ever' day. It's OK."

Gene stepped down from the porch with the uniformed officer and joined the crime scene investigator in the yard. They all stood for a moment watching Garing. The old man reached for his cup on the table and, not finding it, put his hands in his lap and rested his head on his chest. In less than thirty seconds he was asleep.

Gene led the way to the apartment and opened the door using the Yale key. All three officers put on booties and donned nitrile gloves before entering. They left the door open and let the scene investigator lead the inspection.

The apartment was small. The outside door opened into a combination living area and kitchen. A single bedroom was located in the rear with access to a full bath at the rear of the building. The living area contained a small table with four chairs and the investigator indicated those would be dusted for prints. The uniformed officer moved toward the kitchen and carefully opened the refrigerator.

Gene stood in the middle of the room waiting for print dusting to finish before looking at the items on a small bookcase just inside the door. As he was bending over to examine the book titles on the bookcase, he sensed a shadow pass over him from the open door just as a voice came from that same direction.

"Hey! Who are you guys? What are you doing here?"

Gene looked up to see a wiry young man standing in the doorway with an overnight bag at his feet wearing an Army jacket.

""I'm Detective Novalchek from the Cincinnati Police Department. We have a warrant to examine this property. Who are you?"

"I'm Tom Whelan. This is my apartment. What are you doing here?"

CHAPTER 38

In the interrogation room, Tom Whelan looked around at the blank walls. He remembered that the plainclothes policeman at his apartment had said they had been looking for him and someone asked where he had been but then he was warned not to say anything and hustled into a squad car. He knew that his overnight bag had been opened and that one of the uniformed policemen was rummaging through it as he was hustled down the driveway and to the squad car out front. He did not see his landlord, Garing, anywhere about as he was put into the back seat and driven away from the apartment. The trip to police headquarters was accomplished rather quickly and Tom had not had much time to think about what was happening to him or even to puzzle out why he was being arrested.

As he sat, handcuffed to the table in the middle of the room staring at a plate glass wall he wondered about both expected and somewhat odd things like 'why arrest me? I just left town for a while. I'm not AWOL or anything. I did miss some therapy appointments, though. How am I going to go to the toilet handcuffed to this table? I was planning to taking care of that business when I got to the apartment and now I'm shackled like the prisoner of Zenda. For missing some appointments?'

Whelan was tired and had been looking forward to taking a nap went he got home but the whirlwind of activity surrounding his arrest woke him up-but only for a short while. Then his physical tiredness caught up with him and he felt like he couldn't even sit up anymore. He put his head down on the table and rested. Rested physically, at least. He could feel some tension washing out of his tense back and neck muscles and he noted how it had become easier to take a deep breath. But his mind began to spin and wonder more about what the police could be interested in him about, or for. He tried to just relax and not think about his situation, hoping that someone would soon explain the reason for his being detained. But he was not able to keep from constructing a list of potential reasons for his arrest and he found himself putting the list in order of probability to the best of his knowledge. Before he could get all those thoughts together, however, the door burst open with a loud noise. Gene had been watching through the two-way glass and was not going to let his suspect get to sleep.

Gene and Ron entered the room without a word and stared at Tom. He sat up straight in his chair quietly and waited while they slowly walked around him in opposite directions before taking seats in the chairs across the table from him. Whelan suddenly thought, "I don't know the protocol here! What if it's like the silence in haggling over a car price and the next one to speak loses!' He sat up straight and looked at the detectives expectantly, determined to let them explain the situation.

Ron started the conversation. "Tom Whelan, I'm Detective Ron Looney. You've met my partner, Gene Novalchek. Do you know why you are here?"

More than a little relieved that he had not spoken first, Tom licked his lips and said, "I do not, sir."

Neither detective seemed surprised by this statement. Ron opened a folder he had brought in the room and laid on the table. He looked up at Tom and asked, "Are you Staff Sergeant Thomas Whelan?"

"Yes sir."

And your Service number is?"

Tom repeated his number and Ron nodded at the record. "And you currently reside at?"

Tom promptly gave the address where he had been arrested.

"How long have you lived there?"

"Uh, maybe a little more than three months. It's just temporary while I'm in rehab." Suddenly, Tom had a memory about his military training in SERE and about interrogations in general. The rules were to ensure your survival as of first Importance, then to evade capture if possible, but if caught one is to resist, including during interrogation, and lastly try to escape and never give more than a minimum answer. These detectives had not asked why he was in Cincinnati and Tom mentally kicked himself for giving away information.

"And do you know this young woman," Ron asked as he placed a photograph of Margaret Kuykendahl in front of Tom.

Tom examined the photograph and quickly answered, "No, sir. I do not." He determined to answer truthfully and directly but giving only the shortest answer possible.

"Never seen her before?" Gene put in.

"No, sir."

"Can you tell us where you were around midnight on March 26."

"Last week?'

"Yes, around midnight on the 26th." Ron took over the questioning.

"Uh, I was in West Virginia. Sir." For a moment Tom's military attitude slipped.

"Where in West Virginia?"

"Morgantown, sir."

"Are we going to have to get our answers bit by bit or are you going to give us the truth?" Gene interrupted.

"Sorry, sir. I was just answering the question."

"Don't give me that," Gene said getting out of his chair and walking behind Tom. "Where were you in West Virginia that night and what were you doing there?"

"Uh, I was interviewing for a job." Tom turned in his seat to try to face Gene.

"At midnight?" Gene said in a very loud voice.

"Uh, no sir. Earlier that day."

"Where?' nudged Ron.

Tom turned back to face Ron. "I was at the McMaster Self Defense Training Program site in Morgantown."

"Interviewing." Ron let this sound more like a statement than a question.

"That's right, sir."

"Why were you looking for a job, Staff Sergeant?" Ron asked, leaning back in his chair. "You are still active duty, aren't you?'

Tom took a moment to answer and decided he would have to be a little more forthcoming. "I think I'm going to be boarded out of the service and I was looking for employment."

"Why boarded out?"

"I was injured on duty, sir, and my rehab is not going to allow me to return to my previous position."

"Well, that's too bad, Sergeant. What was your previous position?"

"I'm a Ranger, sir."

"Special Operations, then?"

"Yes, sir."

"I see," Ron said this as he made a note in his little book. He finished the note and looked up at Whelan. "Why Morgantown? Aren't there such places around here?"

"Uh, well, yes, sir. But I don't live here. I'm really from Kentucky."

"Uh huh. Then why are you here at all?"

"Rehabilitation, sir. I was injured on active duty and needed convalescent care and rehabilitation."

Ron acted as if he had no prior knowledge of this information. "How did you get injured?"

"On a mission, sir."

"Where?"

"That's really all I can say, sir."

"Huh. We'll come back to that, Sergeant. Can someone back up your story about being in Morgantown?"

"Uh, yes. Sir. There's the Director of Training Operations, Robert Wagoner. I spent the whole day with him and I also met with the Principal, Harvey Monsour. I've got their cards in my bag. There's phone numbers and addresses."

"Are these the cards and the people you are referring to?" Ron asked as he laid the materials out on the table.

Tom took a deep breath, trying to control himself after being told that the police had rifled through his belongings. "Yes sir. They will tell you I was there."

Ron picked up the cards and stood. "We'll see about that."

As he turned toward the door where Gene was waiting to exit with him, Tom interrupted their exit as he spoke up, "Am I under arrest?"

"Just sit still. I'll answer that when I come back," Ron threw his answer over his shoulder as he and Gene left the room.

CHAPTER 39

"What do you think, partner?" Gene asked after the door was securely closed.

"I think we got to check this alibi coming and going. He's got all the markings of being our guy. Right address, Special Operator. But this alibi is quite specific. That could really mess up our case if he's the guy. I'm gonna go check with the people in West Virginia. Why don't you figure out if he could have gotten from there to Cincinnati in time to kill Margaret?

"Gotcha," Gene said and moved off to his desk to pull up some maps and do the calculations.

Ron checked his watch and hurried to his phone to call McMaster Self Defense before they ended their day. He laid the cards down in front of his desk phone and lifted the receiver. As he punched in the ten-digit number for the CEO, or 'Primary' as Whelan had called him, he checked to see that the main number on both men's cards was the same.

"McMaster," came the pleasant voice at the other end.

"This is Detective Ron Looney, Cincinnati Police Department. I'd like to speak with Mr. Monsour, please."

"Certainly, sir. May I tell him the reason for your call?"

Ron wondered if that response was reserved for police inquiries or if she screened everyone that way. "Yes," he replied evenly. "I'm calling about a murder investigation and am checking background references and whereabouts for certain people."

"Oh. Who are you checking on?"

"Right now I'm checking to see if I can speak to Mr. Mansour."

There was a brief pause on the other end of the line and then, "Yes sir. Please hold on."

Ron thought to himself, 'I'm quite sure that's an automatic response but what did she think I was going to do? Hang up? I'm the one that called.'

He replaced the receiver in the cradle after engaging the speakerphone and began sifting thru his notes to ensure he asked the right questions of Mr. Mansour. He had a mental image of Mansour; a thin, balding guy in a pin striped suit, possibly with an English accent. The voice that came on the line did not fit with this picture.

"Hey! Mansour here. What's this about a murder?"

"Mr. Mansour, my name is Ron Lo . . . ."

"Call me Harv. My father is Mr. Mansour. Where you from again?"

"Cincinnati, sir. And I'm calling about . . .

"And none of that 'sir' business either. What's your name again?'

"Ron, Mr. Ma . . . Harv. Just call me Walker.

"Walker, eh? Bet that's got a story behind it, right? Now, what's this about murder all the way over there in Cincinnati?"

"Actually, Harv, I'm calling to confirm whether or not Thomas Whelan was with you on March 26th?"

"Tom Whelan, eh? Yeah, he was here. Quite a story, that young man. Skilled Operator and the country's got a lot of money in him and they're gonna let him go 'cause he can't run stairs two at a time. Damn shame. Good kid. Yes. He was here and I'm gonna offer him a job if the Army keeps up with its damn foolishness. Why do you want to know?"

Ignoring the probe for information, Ron asked another question of his own. "What time was he there in Morgantown, with you on that date, sir, uh, Harv?"

"He was here pretty much the whole day. Came for first interview with Bob at 0900. That's Bob Wagoner, he's the Director of our Training Operations. Bob checks out all the instructor's and drops in on their classes to make sure they do everything right, you know. He's the guy. So any hire we do starts with Bob. He talked with Tom for about an hour and then gave him a tour of our facility. Do you know where we are in Morgantown, Walker?"

"No, I don't." Ron replied, thinking to himself 'and it really doesn't matter where you are in the city, I just want to know when Tom Whelan was there."

"Well, we're out on the east side of the city. We've got several buildings and almost twelve acres of woodland that we can use for our more intense course work."

Feeling like he was about to get a commercial on the McMaster Courses and lose all control of the conversation, Ron quickly inserted, "Did he leave then?"

"Leave? Of course not. After that tour and the interview, Bob thought this was a good candidate for us and he brought him to lunch with the staff. Then I sat down with Staff Sergeant Whelan and we had a very frank discussion about his worth to the Army and I made him promise to let me know if they went ahead with a Disability Board."

"And how long did the two of you talk?"

"Couple of hours, at least. We had a lot of things in common and I wanted him to know . . ."

"Harv, exactly what time did he leave Morgantown?"

"Right. You want to know where he was when this murder occurred. I think he was leaving our campus just a little after 1600. We have a girl on the front desk to handle walk-ins and like that and she leaves at 1600. I seem to remember that she was putting on her coat and waving goodbye as I walked Whelan to the front door."

Trying to truncate the call quickly Ron said, "So you and Bob Wagoner can account for his presence at your place of business from 0900 to 1600 on March 26th?"

"Yes we can. He's a good fellow and I hope this clears up any question about his involvement in whatever is going on over there."

"Thank you very much, Mr. Mansour . . ."

"Harv."

"Harv. This helps us very much. Goodbye."

Ron hit the button to turn off the speaker and slumped back in his chair. He felt like he had run several miles to get the minimum amount of information. And he also became aware of a headache beginning in the back of his head. Was it the teleconference with 'Harv' causing this headache or was he getting low on caffeine? Only one way to tell. Ron looked across the desk and caught his partner's eye and made a motion like drinking from a cup and waved toward the door.

By way of an answer Gene bobbed up and grabbed his jacket and a handful of papers including a map and both headed for the stairs and the coffee shop.

Chapter 40

They had walked silently down the stairs and up the street, each with their own thoughts about the implications of their most recent findings and what to say to each other. Once they had their coffee and were seated at the usual small table in the back of the shop, Ron started the conversation with a quick recital of his interview with Mansour at McMaster Self-Defense Training Program. His presentation of the facts was characteristically short.

"Mansour alibied Whelan for the day of the 26th. Said he left at 4 PM."

However, he then went on to tell Gene about the garrulous Mansour and the unnecessary information he now knew about McMaster and even its location in Morgantown.

Gene listened to this with a small smile threatening to break across his face. He was well aware that, when it came to getting information from people, Ron Looney was both an expert in patiently boring in on key concepts and, at the same time, wanting the person interviewed to adhere to the Joe Friday rule of "just the facts." He also knew that Ron's irritation in this instance compounding the way the interview had gone was because the outcome ran counter to their presumption of Whelan's guilt. He refrained from letting the smile become obvious and waited his turn.

Ron finished his recitation of feeling like he had been subjected to a cross-country run throughout the conversation with Mansour and looked at Gene with eyebrows raised as he took a long draught on his coffee. Gene nodded his understanding both of the facts and the emotion and picked up his own stack of papers. He laid a map of Kentucky and West Virginia in front of Ron and indicated the location of the key points of interest: Morgantown in the northern reaches of West Virginia and directly south of Pittsburgh and Cincinnati straight north of Lexington.

"We've kinda done this before," he said as he traced the major interstate, I-70, west out of Pittsburgh and I-71 from Columbus to Cincinnati. "General estimates are about five hours or a little less to get from Morgantown to Cincinnati."

Both detectives sat for a moment and digested that information while sipping coffee. Again, Ron spoke first. "If he hustled then he sure could make that trip in time to meet Margaret for a late date, right?"

"That's what I'm thinking," Gene said, noticing the lack of enthusiasm on his partner's part. "Was he driving?"

Another pause. "I'm not sure. We didn't actually ask that question."

"Easy enough to do. He's still sitting up in interrogation."

"And we're down here with our coffee. Let's wait just a minute and reconsider things."

Gene lowered his head a bit and looked at his partner under his eyebrows. "Are you buying that alibi and thinking he's not our guy?"

"No. Not completely. Not yet. But think about this, Gene: getting back here in time would be cutting it pretty close. A good defense attorney would have a field day with the timing on this. We need to tighten up that timeline."

"What are you thinking?"

"Well, let's get his story about the drive back. If he went on the interstate and stopped at one of those rest places maybe we can catch him on a camera with a time stamp."

"Or maybe he bought some gas or food on the way."

"Right. Anything at all that can get a time and place we can make that timeline more believable." Ron was draining his cup as he said this.

Gene recognized the signal and endorsed it by finishing his coffee, as well. They stood, nodded to each other in agreement on the plan and left the shop on the way back to the station.

CHAPTER 41

Tom Whelan was right where they had left him, handcuffed to the table in the interrogation room. Shortly after they had left, he had convinced one of the men responsible for watching him to allow him to use the toilet. He then had returned to the interrogation room and fallen asleep on the table.

"He sure looks comfortable, doesn't he?" Gene asked looking into the room before entering.

"You think that's a sign of innocence? Or a clean conscience?" Ron parried.

"Not necessarily. He could be so long on sociopathy that he is never really uncomfortable."

"You getting a degree in something?" Ron looked at Gene.

"Nope. Just doing reading about the criminal element."

"Your day job doesn't give you enough of that? Sometimes I feel like we oughta be writing those books ourselves."

"Yeah. Sometimes I feel that way, too. This isn't one of them, though. Just can't put my finger on it."

"Let's see if he's got the answers for us," Ron said opening the door and entering the room. This time he didn't slam the door open and yet Tom Whelan woke up with their entrance and sleepily looked up at them as he asked, "What's next?"

"We have a few more questions," Ron said.

"About what? I already told you I was in West Virginia. Did you call them?"

"Yes I did," Ron said sitting down and answering Whelan's question sincerely. "And they agreed that you were there. Although that's good news for you, it did raise a couple of other questions for us."

"What? I told you everything already, sir." Whelan was wakening up and returning to his military bearing and answers.

Gene asked, "How did you travel to West Virginia? Were you driving?"

"Yeah. Uh, yes, sir."

"Where'd you get the car? We don't show that you own one."

"I rented it, sir. I believe the receipt is in my duffel bag."

"What route did you travel?" Ron interjected.

"Uh, Interstate all the way. I-71 to Columbus, then I-70 to I-79 directly into Morgantown. Sir."

"How long is that drive," Gene asked almost conversationally.

"It took me a little over six hours, sir."

"Triple A indicates it can be done faster than that."

"Probably. But I had to stop every couple of hours and get out and walk. The hip gets stiff and very uncomfortable with prolonged sitting. I think it was pretty close to six and half hours."

"And all on the Interstate, right?"

"Yes, sir."

Ron changed the subject. "Why Morgantown to look for job? That seems like a fair distance."

"That's right, sir. I would rather have looked closer to home but the Social Worker at New City had been looking around for me and she found this place and noted they had an opening. She actually called and gave them my credentials, well, best as she could, anyway. And they were interested and she set up this interview."

"Kinda quick like, it seems. Is that right?" Gene was still being conversational.

"Well, yes, sir. It was sudden. I was just leaving therapy and she stopped me and told me about the opportunity. We had been talking some after my rehab began to plateau and it looked like I might not get back. To Operations, you know."

Again Ron jumped in to change the subject. "How do you get along with the other members of your team?"

"You mean the Rangers?"

"That's right. You get along with them? Everybody and everything copasetic?"

Whelan allowed himself a small grin. "Absolutely, sir. Couldn't have it any other way. Each of us on the team depends on each of the others to have our back at all times. Can't be any other way."

"How about the team leader? You get on with him?"

"Master Sergeant Mickelson? Absolutely. Everyone on the squad looks up to Mick."

Ron sat quietly for a few moments staring at Whelan who sat, back straight in the chair and looked back at Ron. There was no evidence that Tom could see of insolence or arrogance in the look and he ultimately just briefly nodded at Whelan and got up to leave the room.

"Are we finished, sir? May I return to the apartment now?"

"No. We are not done yet. You'll be our guest tonight," Ron said without rancor. He and Gene met outside after securing the door.

Gene said, "I still say he could have made that trip in time to be our doer."

Ron slowly shook his head. "Even though I think you're right about that, there's something here that doesn't quite add up."

"What?"

"Well, you weren't with me when I talked to Scooter. He's the only one who has seen "TJ" face-to-face. He gave me a very different picture of the guy than what I'm seeing in there." He indicated the interrogation room.

"Can we get him in for an ID?"

"Oh, Ah, no, that's not going to happen. I guess I didn't tell you in the fuss about catching Whelan. Scooter was executed by the mob after he left the precinct. We have no eyewitness. Listen, I need to talk with Bolling about this Social Worker referral anyway. I'll see if the therapists agree with Scooter about "TJ" being a mean SOB. If he has any tendency in that regard it ought to have come out during rehab."

"I'll get him moved to a cell," Gene said starting down the hall, leaving Ron standing and wondering whether Tom Bolling would be at home on in his truck at this time of evening.

CHAPTER 42

Tom Bolling was in his truck on his way home from New City Hospital. Tom was quite proud of his truck, a five-year old Ford F-150, black with red racing stripe and a matte black UWS Low Profile Tool Box in the bed. Tom was a retired USAF Brigadier General orthopedic surgeon and his toolbox was well equipped with emergency medical supplies in addition to emergency roadside equipment like a heavy car jack, pry bar, jumper cables and a set of wrenches and screwdrivers. Tom particularly liked the height advantage the truck gave him over the rest of the drivers on the road; he tended to think of them as 'competition' and wanted the ability to see far ahead to take advantage of traffic patterns.

Tom had left the hospital a little later than usual because of his need to get through a pile of paperwork on his desk. None of it was truly emergency type work but Tom had a policy of 'doing today's work today' and knew he would be more at ease at home with the knowledge that the paperwork was completed. He knew the possibilities of intervening crises in a hospital work environment was high and might prevent him from doing the work first thing in a day. So he always left his desk clear of work and that day there had been several requests for new operating privileges sent to him by the Credentialing Committee so he stayed and finished his review.

As the chief of staff at New City, Tom had administrative responsibilities ranging from recruitment of physician staff to organizing the hospital's performance improvement plan and assuring that all accrediting bodies were satisfied with the work done by New

City. And, since last year, he had become the *de facto* backup for the Public Affairs Officer, Johnny Taliaferro, for dealing with problems in the newspaper. Prior to that time, the hospital director, Sam Mastone had wanted to be the face of the hospital in such events. After Tom had bailed the hospital out of potentially bad publicity over a murder, however, Sam had quietly told Tom to deal with such problems; he intended to continue to be seen at ribbon cutting and other ceremonies, nonetheless.

Tom was not dwelling on any of these issues as he drove. He was simply looking forward to a night at home, quiet dinner and a little reading in the company of his wife, Susan. So, he was rather mellow when he took Ron's call.

"What's up Razorback?" he queried. Both he and Ron Looney had Arkansas heritage and upbringing in common in addition to their shared experience in the Air Force.

"You driving?"

"Yes, that's how I usually get home in the evenings."

"Well, be safe and just listen."

"Ron, I've got you on speaker and both hands on the wheel."

"Try listening harder. Sounds like you're talking."

"I could be hanging up now."

"Not yet. I need a favor."

"Just like almost every other time you call me."

"Yeah, well, I'm a needy guy."

"What do you need?"

"A little more on that Whelan guy, two things actually."

"Did you find him?"

"Yes we did, in a way. Actually he walked in on us searching his place."

"Well, that's handy. What do you need from me if you already have him?"

"First, he said he was out of town in West Virginia on the date in question and that was because your social worker got him an interview back there. I appreciate it if you could talk to the appropriate people and clear that up for me."

"You mean confirm his alibi?"

"You may be watching too many crime movies. I just want that part of the story confirmed, or not. That's all."

"OK, Ron. I can do that. First thing in the morning."

"Great. And then there's this other little thing . . ."

"First the slow windup and then the fast ball."

"No. It's not like that. Just hear me out."

"Go on. But don't make it a long story. I'm getting off the Interstate and I'll be home in a few."

"Here's the question. The guy we're looking for is called "TJ" and is known in the criminal circles to have a mean streak. This guy Whelan seems like a straight arrow. All 'yes, sir' and 'no, sir' with us and I need to know if he's real or not."

"And you want me to make that decision for you?"

"No. No. I'd like you to ask those therapists about his base personality. I'm thinking a mean streak is most liable to come out when there's pain or somebody egging you on. Far as I know that's standard operating procedure in physical therapy. That's why we call 'em 'physical terrorists', right?"

"Don't say that in front of them or we'll both be in pain," Tom laughed.

"So, can you talk to someone who saw him in therapy and get me an opinion?"

"Yes, of course I can. Maybe I can even get that for you first thing, too."

"You're a good man, Tom Bolling. No matter what all those other people say about you."

"And as far as I know, there's no one even saying that about you."

"Well, you're not down here at the precinct. Everyone here thinks I'm a great guy."

"Anyway, 'Great Guy', I just pulled up in my driveway. You'll hear from me tomorrow."

"Nice doing business with you, General."

"Don't call me. I'll call you, Master Sergeant."

Chapter 43

R on hung up the phone and looked around the Dick Pen; no one was there. He shrugged and leaned back in his chair and thought about his plan for dealing with Meg's absence. Their daughter, Kate, was due for delivery of her first child-and the Looney's first grandchild-in Helena, Montana. Katie's husband, Jon was a professor of business at Carroll College there, teaching Marketing. Katie was a junior staffer for the Speaker of the House in the Montana Legislature. Now that she was due to deliver, Meg had flown to Helena and would not be back until Momma and Baby were safely home and well into a new schedule.

That meant that Ron was on his own for meals and the like. "Batching it' was not strange to him, as he had cared for himself in terms of laundry, meals and housekeeping for several years before he and Meg had married. The issue at this time in Ron's mind, however, was that in Meg's absence there was no one to sense his need for a home-cooked chicken dinner before thinking his way through the maze and dead-ends of this case. That fried chicken dinner routine of Meg's, coming when she recognized Ron's perplexity and frustration over a case, had helped him winnow through a lot of chaff and get to the meat of a case more than once.

Once, when he had been bedeviled by conflicting details of a case at the same time he was in some personal conflict with one of the Associate District Attorneys, Ron had asked Meg to call out the chicken dinner routine. And the routine failed him, miserably. He learned the lesson that Meg had to sense the time for the magic dinner, not him.

However, Ron remembered that before he met Meg, his habit of sitting in a small little West German bar sipping on a beer for hours had been useful in helping him to think through the inconsistencies in a case and, after a good night's sleep, see the case and the principals in a very different light. Ron did not want to go bar hopping so he had another plan. He was going to 'recognize' his need for a special time and special meal and then go make that meal himself.

He grabbed his coat from the back of his chair and walked to the garage, waved goodnight to the duty officer and got in his car. His first stop was the famous southern fried chicken drive-through where he ordered a three-piece meal with mashed potatoes and green beans and a side of cornbread. With the meal on the passenger seat he found the small grocery store close to his home and bought a six-pack of Over-The-Rhine Ale.

At home, he carefully unloaded the food and drink, locked the car and the house, hung up his jacket and opened the first of the OTR long-neckers. Ron knew what he was doing in the kitchen and soon had a formal place setting on the dining room table and the carryout food in serving dishes. But the arrangement and the pretense could not fool his taste buds. "Nothing like Meg's." he thought as he took his first bite of chicken. "And not even close to what Momma could do," he reminisced with the second bite.

The meal did not improve in his opinion as he went on through the green beans and the mashed potatoes. He wondered how a business could stay in the black when their mashed potatoes were far less tasty than wallpaper paste. He threw a large pat of butter on the pile of potatoes and re-heated them in the microwave. At least then they tasted like greasy wallpaper paste. The cornbread crumbled in his hand as he tried to butter it and he decided that was a bridge too far. The cornbread and the remaining potatoes were scooped into the garbage.

But he finished the chicken, rinsed the dishes and realized he had forgotten dessert. Meg always had a hot apple pie with cheddar cheese on his piece at the end of her famous meal. He rummaged around in the refrigerator and found some Swiss cheese slices and ate two of those. But it clearly wasn't the same.

He took another beer to the living room, and opened his record cabinet. Ron had a large collection of leading jazz and blues artists and their major albums. He selected an album by Thelonious Monk and another by Ahmed Jamal to put on the turntable. Just as he was about to close the cabinet, he noticed an album his son, Kent had given to him on his last birthday party. Kent said, "Try it out Dad, you can always turn it off."

The album featured The Doors. Ron spun it in his hands for a bit and then put it on the record changer with the others. He set the volume low, like he always did. He claimed that was to keep from disturbing Meg, but the deeper truth was Ron didn't really like loud music.

Once everything was arranged for his support, Ron sat on the couch and opened his briefcase to empty the contents on the coffee table. He spent the next hour arranging materials in different order on the tabletop. Sometimes he got up and moved to the other side of the table to examine information from a new perspective. As the evening wore on and there were no revelations or new insights, Ron more often went to the refrigerator for another beer.

After several hours he actually went to sleep on the couch and was awakened by The Doors playing 'Roadhouse Blues' at a volume he didn't expect. He turned the volume down and stretched and went to get the last beer. He opened the refrigerator and realized that he had already gotten the last beer before he went to sleep.

Ron looked at he clock on the microwave which said, unbelievably, that the night was now gone and the time was nearing 1:00 AM. A quick review of events reminded him of a poor dinner, absent dessert, disappearing beer and a resounding lack of progress on his case. He decided that his bright idea wasn't really all that bright so he packed up the materials back into his briefcase and went upstairs to bed.

CHAPTER 44

R on was trudging up the back stairs at the precinct when Tom's call came. After his short night and restless sleep, Ron was startled by the loudness of the ringer and stopped in the stairwell to answer. He checked the name on the caller ID took a deep breath and put some extra joviality into his voice.

"Well, Big Doc, first thing is the first thing. I'm not even at my desk yet. What have you got for me?"

"Well, Big Detective, you should know that surgical cases usually start at 7:30 each morning and we have a lot to do before that. Did you have a nice big breakfast?"

"C'mon, Tom, don't give me that 'working surgeon' story here. We all know you turned in your scalpel for a fountain pen."

"I'm still here early and you know it. I talked with the social worker. She had done some counseling with Whelan after his rehab began to miss the mark he set for getting back to the Ranger Unit. He had a little depression but was willing to consider another career. She had taken the initiative and found this opening in Morgantown and set up an interview before telling him about it."

"But he went, didn't he?"

"Yes, but you already knew that. Your question was whether the interview appointment was something he did, like maybe to seem like he was out of town?

"Well, yes, that was a big part of it. Also just wanted to know if I was getting a snow job. Did this social worker think he was a mean and nasty kinda guy?"

"She certainly did not. Further I took your suggestion and checked with the therapist who worked the most with him in rehab. Becca said he was not only a nice person; he tried to make jokes about everything. She went so far as to say that if you're looking for a 'mean, bad actor' you are not looking for Tom Whelan."

"Be that as it may, we have a fairly strong circumstantial case against him right now. And we have a video of him walking with the girl just shortly before she was murdered."

"Becca says she would like to view that video. She knows Whelan pretty well and she can give you a positive identification if that's what you need."

"Well, that couldn't hurt," Ron said a little pensively. "When could you guys look at it if I got it brought it over there now?"

"We're here and available at any time. Probably the earlier the sooner, though. That's the way things are in a hospital."

"I'll be there in less than half an hour."

CHAPTER 45

R on and Gene walked through the lobby at New City and noted the mid-morning pause of coffee drinkers at the Green Bean kiosk. Nick looked up nodded to Ron.

"We don't get this kind of chance often," Ron said and he and Gene veered over to the kiosk. "Hey, Nick. Let me have two of my 'usuals'."

"When did you get so regular over here that you've got your own 'usual' coffee drink," Gene asked with both eyebrows raised.

"Been with you most times, haven't I?" came the response.

"But we've never had a 'usual' that I can remember."

"I was out her to see Tom with the drawing and Nick decided I needed a 'usual'. Don't worry. It's like Sandy and the 'usual' we get from her at lunch."

"If only. This better be good."

"Don't worry about it partner. I'm buying. This time."

They got their drinks and Ron paid the cashier. Both men waved their thanks to Nick and headed for the Executive Suite.

"Hey, this is really good," Gene, said after one sip. "Really strong, but good. Nice and smooth. What's it called?"

"It's my 'usual'. I thought you heard that."

Mary Brighthouse, Tom Bolling's secretary, smiled at them when they entered and said, "He's waiting for you in his office."

Tom greeted them as they entered and introduced a slim woman in her mid 20s with deep auburn hair. "This is Rebecca Fletcher. She is one of our therapists and was the one primarily working with Whelan."

"Nice to meet you, Ms Fletcher," Gene said.

Ron asked, "Are you the one that identified Whelan from our artist's sketch?"

"Yes, sir. That was me," she said. "But Tom Whelan is not mean or nasty. I know that, too."

"I appreciate your interest and energy in this case, Ms Fletcher. We want your input but mostly, right now we want you to take a look at this video and see if that's Tom Whelan walking down the street."

"Where's this from?" she asked.

"Really not important," Ron answered. "We just want your opinion on this man."

Tom had arranged for a video playback machine to be connected to a television screen in his office for the viewing. Gene pulled the disc with the recording out of its folder and inserted it in the machine. Almost immediately the screen was filled with static and flickering lines but they promptly coalesced into a street scene. The scene was centered on the near sidewalk from a distance of about ten feet. The bottom of the scene was a floored cubicle and the top showed the street and the far sidewalk with a few feet of the storefronts across the street.

As the group watched, a couple strode into view on the far sidewalk. They were holding hands and facing each other, talking. The man was on the outside, closest to the camera and his face was not clearly seen. The woman's face appeared every few steps and was clearly Margaret Kuykendahl. Ron and Gene had watched this video more than thirty times and instead of watching it again, they watched the faces of Tom Bolling and Rebecca Fletcher.

The stroll of the couple on the tape lasted only a few seconds before the flickering static reappeared. The detectives looked at the medical personnel questioningly. "What did you see?" Ron asked.

Tom shook his head but Rebecca said, "I'd like to see that again, please."

In the end they played it for her 10 times in total. Twice she asked them to play it at half speed. Then she turned to Tom and said, "Dr. Bolling, I really can't see that man's face very well but I do know Tom Whelan's limp. He has an injured hip socket and his limp is a hip-related limp involving the left leg. The man in that video is limping from a knee injury involving his right knee. That's not Tom Whelan. I know the way he walks and that isn't him."

Gene and Ron both turned to stare at Tom who leaned forward and replayed the video again first at normal speed and then at half-speed. He looked up at Ron and said, "Becca's right. That limp is from a knee injury and it favors the right side. We know Tom Whelan has a left hip injury. He wouldn't walk like that."

Gene wanted clarity and asked, "So you're saying this is absolutely not Tom Whelan?"

Both Tom Bolling and Rebecca Fletcher nodded.

Ron had been partly expecting some controversy over the interpretation of the video but not an absolute denial of the man's identity. He felt like all the air had been sucked out of the room. His plan to test the possibility of Whelan getting from Morgantown to Cincinnati in time to murder Margaret suddenly seemed rather trivial. He smiled at Tom and Rebecca, collected the disc and he and Gene left New City with a new headache.

CHAPTER 46

The trip back to the precinct was relatively quiet although each of them said, at one time or another, "That means the guy we've got isn't our killer." And each time that was said, the other one agreed and silence ensued for several minutes.

"I feel like this guy has been leading us on," Gene said when they were about to re-interview him. "I mean if he isn't our guy, why do I feel like he's not telling us everything?"

"I have that feeling that something isn't right there, too. But let's talk to him differently and see what we can get."

Whelan was brought up from Holding and put back into the interrogation room. He had slept in his clothes and he was rumpled and needed a bath. But he sat upright in the chair and faced them as they entered.

"Are you ready to let me go now?" he asked before they got seated.

"Not just yet. We have a couple of additional questions. Things that are still bothering us about your story," Ron said, taking the lead.

"Such as what? I think I've answered all you questions."

"Well, how about this Mr. Whelan: if you left Morgantown at 4:00 PM on the 26th of March, why were you just getting back to your apartment yesterday?"

"I didn't say I left Morgantown at 4:00PM, I left the McMaster Center at that time."

"And went where?"

"I stayed at a small motel nearby."

"You stayed the night in Morgantown?" Gene's voice got somewhat louder at this news.

"Yes."

"Why? Too tired to drive back?"

"No. Mr. Wagoner had offered me a chance to participate in some of their classes the next morning and I decided to stay and do so."

"You were back at McMaster the following morning?" "Yes, sir."

"What time did you arrive?" Ron wanted to know,

"The exercises started at 0700 and I was there shortly beforehand."

"When did you leave Morgantown, then?"

"About mid afternoon. I drove from there to Wheeling where I have some cousins and I stayed there a couple of days until yesterday when I drove back."

"You were in West Virginia from early in the morning on March 26 until day before yesterday?" Ron asked in a rather stunned voice.

"Yes, sir."

"Why didn't you tell us this when we first talked to you?" Ron's voice was getting a little louder; Gene couldn't sit at the table any longer and got up to pace around.

"Sir, I just answered your questions. You asked about my whereabouts on March 26. I just told you where I was. That's all I knew that you wanted to know."

Ron turned to look at Gene who shrugged and left the room. Ron collected the information about Whelan's relatives in Wheeling including their phone numbers and also left, shaking his head.

CHAPTER 47

Ron sat at his desk and thought about the recent events and the strong implication that Tom Whelan was not the 'TJ" he and Gene were seeking. He briefly considered that he and Gene had been the subject of a Jedi mind trick with everyone saying, "this is not the man you are seeking". After a few moments he picked up the phone and called West Virginia.

"McMaster," came the familiar voice in Morgantown.

"This is Detective Ron Looney, Cincinnati Police Department. I'd like to speak with Mr. Monsour, please."

"Certainly, sir. May I tell him the reason for your call?"

Ron wondered if the woman asked that routinely or if she had actually forgotten that he had called the day before.

"Yes," he answered. "I still need to talk to him about a murder investigation.

Once again there was a brief pause on the other end of the line and then she said, "Yes sir. Please hold on." And he was placed on hold.

Mansour answered within two minutes and opened with, "Well, detective, how's your case going now. Turns out it wasn't our boy Tom, I hope."

"It may very well turn out that way. Especially since I now find out that he spent not only the 26th with you but was back there early on the 27th to take part in some training."

"Absolutely right. He's a good man, I told you that. Came in for the first class. Early morning. Showed us some very good form and skill here with a class of students. He was very good at the teaching, too. Patient and helpful to the slow ones. Even Bob isn't very good at that. I want to hire Tom."

"All well and good, Harv. Why didn't you tell me he stayed over and was back at your place early the next morning?"

"What? I don't recall you asking about anything other than whether he was here on the 26th. I think you were pretty clear about that and exactly what time he left us at the end of that day. The 26th. I'm pretty sure you didn't ask about any other days."

"And you didn't think that might be important?"

"No sir. My cooperation with the authorities is simple and straightforward. I answer all questions truthfully."

Ron thought, 'Truthfully perhaps but with a lot of opinion and bluster.' But he didn't say that. Instead, he told Mansour, "Well, it looks more and more like Tom Whelan will be available for you to hire in the near future. Thanks for your help.

"Certainly. Glad to be of assistance. That's what we do here. We teach people to be of assistance, first to themselves and then to anyone else who may need their help. We're proud of our work here and glad that you think Tom can be available to join us."

Again feeling like he was in a contest of words, Ron quickly said, "That will be his decision, of course. But I don't think there will be a legal impediment to you offering him a job. Goodbye." And then he quickly hung up.

He turned to Gene and commented, "Confirmation on Whelan being back in Morgantown early on the 27th. That and the statement by Rebecca seems to put Whelan in the clear."

Gene scratched his head. "If so, how did we get so wrapped around the axle here? We were looking for a military-like guy with Special Ops training and a limp that lived in that neighborhood. Whelan fits every one of those criteria."

"He sure does," Ron agreed, "but you got to admit that the video identification of "its not Whelan" and having to pack a round trip from Morgantown to Cincinnati for a killing date between 4:00 PM on the 26th and 7:00 AM on the 27th is pushing it."

"Still believe it could be done."

"Technically, I agree. But I have a lot of trouble with him being able to 'patiently' spend a half day teaching self-defense moves after such a trip."

"You know what this means?"

"You talking about if he's not our guy?"

"Of course."

"Yes. I understand that puts us back to square one."

"Aren't you uncomfortable doing that?"

"There's an old Plains Indian saying that goes, 'If your horse dies, dismount.' And I think we just saw our horse die."

"Still . . ."

"No, Gene. We need to put on our big boy pants and go apologize."

CHAPTER 48

Their entry into the interrogation room was very different from previous. Gene and Ron were slow in coming in, closed the door quietly behind them and sat across the table from Tom Whelan with small smiles and some difficulty in meeting his gaze.

Tom felt that the atmosphere had changed but was uncertain what that meant so he refrained from asking questions. He sat quietly and looked from one to the other.

Ron opened the discussion. "Mr. Whelan, we have confirmed your alibi for the 26th and 26th of March."

"It wasn't an alibi. I really was there. What did you think I was doing?"

"Mr. Whelan, we are investigating the murder of a young woman . . ."

"That the one whose picture you showed me?"

"Yes. That's right. We have every belief that someone living in the area where you have your apartment killed her. And we believe that person is military trained in Special Operations and walks with a limp."

"Oh . . ."

"That's why you were brought in. That's why we were so specific about your whereabouts on the evening on March 26. You really fit all the particulars of the person we were seeking."

"But I didn't have anything to do with killing that girl. I don't even know her."

"We didn't know that at the beginning of our . . . discussions with you. But the people at McMaster have confirmed that you were there on both the 26th and 27th, so . . ."

"You don't think I drove over here that night?"

"No, we don't. Although it is possible to do so, we have other good reasons to think that the person we saw with the woman who was killed was not you."

"You saw this guy?"

"Well, we have a video of him and her from across the street but we couldn't see his face. Until very recently we had reason to believe that was you in the video. Now we don't think that was you."

"But you thought he was military. Why?"

"Mr. Whelan, this is an ongoing investigation and we do not reveal certain particulars about the case during the investigation."

"Even if I might could help you?"

"What are you talking about?"

"There is a guy I met just before I left for West Virginia. I think he's in rehab, too. At least, that's where we met. We had coffee together after a session."

"What else can you tell us about him?"

"He said he was Navy. A Seal, and said he hurt his knee in an operation. Just like me. Said he had just arrived in Cincinnati and was staying in a motel outside of town and he asked if I knew some place with cheaper rates. He seemed like a genuine nice guy and I told him he could use my place for a week or so while I was back east. He could look around for a better place during that time and . . ."

"Wait a minute. This guy with Special ops training was living in your apartment that week?" Gene could hardly sit still. He twisted in his chair and looked at his partner before asking, "What was this guy's name?"

"I don't really know . . ."

Both detectives visibly slumped at this.

"He just said to call him 'TJ' like some kind of nickname."

The silence in the room was profound. Ron turned to Gene and said, "Like you said, all the particulars, just the wrong guy."

Then he turned to Whelan and said, "That's very good information, Mr. Whelan. I appreciate you telling us this. Can I ask why you didn't tell us this before now?"

Whelan looked at Ron and his eyebrows came together in a puzzled face. "I didn't know what you were looking for until just now. You never asked me about anyone else. All your questions were about me and where I was, not someone else."

Ron looked at Gene and said, "At least we're very consistent."

CHAPTER 49

"So, where do we go from here, partner?" Gene asked with a touch of sarcasm.

"Well, you know the drill. Let's do something so we don't think we're doing nothing. First let's release Whelan. Then we spend the day writing up why we latched on to him in the first place."

"And we change our terminology back to the original."

"What are you talking about?"

"I mean, we have to start calling our perp 'TJ' again, right?" "Oh yeah. That's right. But of course we now know that he is limping on his right knee and not on his left hip injury."

"Right. That's a big improvement in our description. Probably going to lead us right to him."

Ron looked at his partner and smiled wryly. Now that the drug activity had been upset with Walt Matthews' raid the gang was probably long gone from Cincinnati. They had lost their drug stash and probably most of their money. No one could imagine any reason for any of them to hang around in the area.

And with the gang's disappearance, 'TJ' was also likely gone. Nothing was good about that in the eyes of the detectives.

Ron started on the paperwork to release Tom Whelan and Gene started gathering their information together focusing on 'TJ' and removing what was clearly related to Tom Whelan, They sat and worked quietly for half an hour. Whelan was released and his belongings were returned. Ron arranged to have a black and white take him back to his apartment.

A little later Gene looked up and said, "Coffee?" and they left the building for the coffee shop.

Sipping their respective drinks at their favored table in the back, Gene commented, 'This 'usual' doesn't taste like the one Nick made."

"According to Tom, Nick is an Italian trained expert professional barista. Of course his drinks taste better."

"When I was growing up we didn't even know that barista was a real job. If I had heard that term growing up I would have thought it referred to a girl working in a bar."

Ron nodded without answer.

Gene continued, "When is Meg coming back? You are getting to be less and less of a conversationalist every day."

"Oh, sorry. I'm just thinking what we can tell the Kuykendahl's. We've run ourselves all over the city chasing the wrong limp and now their daughter's killer has left our jurisdiction."

"Maybe they'll understand."

"Would you? Would you understand why the police couldn't catch your daughter's killer?"

Gene nodded but said, "It happens. You know it happens. We hear about 'cold cases' all the time. We'll put this out on the wire. Somebody in the next city will recognize the Special Operator with a limp and we can still get him."

"Maybe." Ron was silent for another minute, and then said, "Not sure when Meg's coming back. Katie should have delivered by now but she's not even having contractions. And Meg's gonna stay for about a week after the delivery."

"Listen, Sandy's not available tonight so we're both batching it. Let's go have a steak and beer somewhere."

Ron nodded as he finished his coffee. "That sounds good to me. Even if I'm playing second fiddle to Sandy. Where do you want to go?"

"Let's do Blinkers"

"Really? You want to leave the city?"

"It's just across the bridge, all the other steak houses are farther out."

"You're a persuasive devil, Gene Novalchek."

"Funny. That's what Sandy always says."

Later, after a large medium rare steak, salad and baked potato, they sat with a final cup of coffee and relaxed for perhaps the first time in days.

Gene noted, "This is the time my dad would pull out a big cigar and offend everyone in sight by firing up and blowing the smoke straight up."

"Yep, End of the meal ritual. Happened at my house, too. Only Dad would go out on the front porch to smoke. He'd sit in that rocking chair, light up that stubby stem pipe and close his eyes like he'd gone to heaven."

Gene was silent for a minute. Then, "Your Dad still OK?"

Ron nodded. "Yeah. Still dealing with the paralysis, but like I said he walks the yard before bedtime every night."

"He still smoking that pipe?"

Ron laughed before answering, "No. He can't get anyone to help him."

That comment puzzled Gene, "Help him do what?'

Ron put both his hands on the table and indicated them as he talked, "See, my Dad always told us boys that he had a clean record with the police and he thought that was because he was a pipe smoker. He told us that a pipe smoker didn't have time for 'no foolishness' as he put it. My Grandma would have said something about 'idle hands'."

"I don't get it," Gene said, leaning back and preparing for one of his partners winding stories of lowland Arkansas wisdom.

"Well, according to my Dad, no real pipe smoker would ever have 'idle hands'. First those hands are patting his clothing and checking in all pockets just to find the pipe itself. Then those hands get involved in another pat-down looking for the pipe tools."

"There are pipe tools?"

"Oh man, are there tools. First you have to have a reamer to clean out the char and old tobacco in the pipe bowl. Then, often you would want to run a pipe cleaner through the stem to clean out the tar and stuff. And rarely are those tools kept in the same pocket so there's another set of pocket patting exercises to go through. And once you've got that done and before you can go any further, you've got to put those tools back in a pocket somewhere. Then you go thru the search process all over again to locate where you put the tobacco pouch."

"Man, I'm tired already."

"Oh, listen, we are not through by a long shot. After you find it, you unroll the tobacco pouch and you smell the tobacco and put a finger in it to assure yourself it's not too dry. Then comes the pipe packing: stick the bowl down in the tobacco and start feeding small amounts of tobacco into it, just a little at a time and packing it down with your finger. And you continue this part of the ritual until it is "just so". Too tight and it won't stay lit and too loose and it's all gone too soon. Once you get the packing just right, the pipe comes out and you have to close the pouch and put it somewhere, back in a pocket or maybe on the table while you start the search for a light, matches if you're a farmer like Dad or maybe a fancy lighter if you're a banker or something like that."

"Well, you are correct, sir. That takes a lot of time."

"Hold on. We're not through. To light the pipe is also a careful process. You must hold the flame at a right angle to the bowl and carefully puff on the stem to suck the flame down into the bowl. And the puffing is time and depth sensitive; the first couple puffs are short and quick to heat the tobacco and then you use slower, deeper pulls on the stem to draw the flame well into the bowl to get an even light. Do this incorrectly and the bowl won't stay lit."

"That is very tedious and almost scientific."

"What? You think we're done? That's just got us started. After one or two puffs the pipe smoker starts through his pockets again looking for the tamping tool."

"Still another tool?"

"Oh yeah. This one has a large flat head, about the size of the end of a double-A battery. The smoker now uses this tool to tamp down the burning tobaccos to distribute the fire evenly and keep the pipe lit, he hopes. But the fact is, pipes keep going out and the smoker has to re-light, sometimes remove some of the top burned tobacco, always have to re-tamp. And, if the smoker gets involved in a conversation and forgets to pay attention to the stupid pipe, it will go out again.

"Why in the world would anyone go through all that?"

"I asked Dad about that once. His answer was 'for the fun of it'. And it really does smell good. But it's also expensive."

"I can see that. All them tools and stuff."

"More than that. A real pipe smoker has to have several pipes and a place to keep them. If you smoke a pipe, you don't have time to get in trouble."

"But you don't smoke, do you, Ron?"

"Nope, and I never did. Makes you cough and your clothes smell like your house was on fire."

CHAPTER 50

T he next day, Captain Arne Thorason greeted Ron as he entered the Dick Pen and was headed for his office. "No luck, huh?"

"No, sir. Seems likely the whole team split after Walt's raid took out their stash and their cash."

"Need you on a new case, then." The Captain's terse wording did not convey disappointment about the Margaret Kuykendahl case; it was simply his way to conserve words.

"What's it about?"

"Found a DB over near the Race St. Station," Thorason said, mentioning one of the ancient subway stations on Cincinnati's long-abandoned subway.

"In or out?" Ron asked as Gene came in the office and hung his coat on the hanger he kept by his desk.

Thorason nodded to Gene and went on, "Out, but he might've been in. That's the thing. Check it out."

"Right away, Cap'n" Ron said, as he signaled Gene to put his jacket back on.

They went to the stairway and Ron said over his shoulder as they descended, "We got to go get coffee to go. I didn't realize that we were out of coffee at home."

"Fine with me. I'd like a Morning Bun, too."

On the way to the coffee shop, Ron told Gene what little information he had learned from the Captain about the body at Race St. Station. They wondered and even considered various possibilities until they got to the scene.

The Race St. 'Station' is an enclosed area at ground level on the corner of Race Street and 4th Street. The 'station' was intended to have been one of the access points to Cincinnati's subway system nearly 100 years before. Now it is the empty space in a large vacant building closed off from public access. The patrol car at the scene was blocking access to the corner on Fourth Street and the uniformed officer had protected the area around the corner with crime scene tape. At the corner of the building was the body. It was a middle-aged man in a heavy overcoat slumped up against the corner as if sleeping. He had unkempt hair and clothing, was unshaven for days and presented a smell that mixed alcohol, marijuana and body odor in a most unappealing way.

"Anybody touch anything?" Gene asked as they approached.

The uniformed cop answered, "Not since I got here. Maybe twenty minutes."

"Any witnesses?" Ron asked

"Some guys standing around when I got here said they were just passing and saw him. Thought he was asleep."

"Did they roust him?"

"Said they didn't but that was before I got here."

"You got their names?"

"Yes, sir. Right here," he indicated his left front shirt pocket.

Gene used his ballpoint pen to open the dead man's coat and examine the body for evidence of trauma. When he saw none he tried the inner pockets of the heavy coat but came up empty.

"No obvious identification, Ron."

"Anything suspicious?'

"Does smell count? Because this smell is very suspicious. He may have just died from smelling himself."

"Nothing to go on?"

"Nothing I can see from here."

Ron turned back to the uniformed cop. "Did you call the ME?"

"Uh, no. I thought that was something you guys would do."

"Well, do it now, will you?"

As they waited for the Medical Examiner to arrive the detectives watched a small but steady flow of people from the nearby hotels and apartment buildings walk around their scene in order to get to the Starbucks a block away. Gene held up his travel cup and nodded in the direction of the Starbucks. "We could of gotten our coffee at the scene."

"I told you. I didn't have any at home. I couldn't wait."

"Right. Any news from Montana?"

"Meg says the doctor told Katie she was progressing, whatever that means."

"But no Meg until after the baby, right?"

"Right,"

"Maybe we can do another steak night."

"Right now I just need something to get that smell out of my nose."

The ME arrived with an ambulance right behind her. Dr. Darringer exited her car and retrieved her bag from the back seat. As she turned toward the crime scene she wrinkled her nose and said to Ron, "This had better be worth it."

"Just doing our job, m'am."

"What do we have?" she asked setting her bag down next to the body and reaching in her pocket to get some menthol to apply to her upper lip.

"Best we can tell it's a homeless guy who smoked and drank and died," Gene offered.

"Any obvious wounds?"

"Not that we could see without moving him. We decided to wait for you." Ron thought to himself 'and maybe wait for the smell to disappear, too.'

Darringer stooped next to the body and opened the man's coat and then moved around him to examine what she could without moving the body or undressing it. When she stood up a few minutes later she indicated to her assistant to take some pictures and get the body in the ambulance and then walked over to Ron and Gene.

"I think this may be natural," she said.

"Oh, there is nothing natural about that smell," Gene offered.

Darringer smiled at him and said, "Nonetheless the cause of death is certainly not obvious from my quick external examination. Let me get him back on my table in the lab and I can tell a lot more."

"OK, doc. You'll call if we need to attend?"

"Sure. I don't blame you for wanting to stay away. I expect this one will use up my whole year's budget for odor eaters."

Gene's eyebrows went up.

Ron laughed. "She's talking about those boxes of baking soda we see on her shelves."

Darringer winked at Looney and left.

Ron collected the names of possible witnesses from the officer and he and Gene returned to the office. They spent an hour writing up the case and then sat and talked about Margaret until lunchtime.

Gene wanted to drive but Ron reminded him that if he took his car then Ron would be left with Sandy while Gene went to get the car. So, Ron drove. They each had 'the usual' and Gene spent an extra ten minutes with Sandy after they had paid their checks.

The afternoon was so quiet that they made two trips to the coffee shop, never even bothering to see if the pot in the break room was empty.

That evening Ron called Meg in Helena to find out that Katie was having some contractions but was not progressing and Meg was likely to be out west for another week or so. He told her about running out of coffee and what all he had purchased at the grocery store on the way home. They said they missed each other and went to bed.

Ron intended to sleep in a little on Saturday morning and did not set his alarm. Accordingly, when the loud jangling of the telephone began at 6:15 that morning it came as a very rude awakening. Ron turned over in the bed and grabbed his cell phone from the nightstand.

"Walker," he croaked.

"Hey Ron, this is Walt. We've got something going on you should probably be involved in."

"What's going on?"

"Somebody hit the New City Hospital Pharmacy in the middle of the night. Took a bucket load of narcotics, including fentanyl. I have a sneaking suspicion our guys didn't leave town and they're here trying to get one more deal done. You in?"

Ron was already pulling on his pants. "Absolutely," he said, hanging up abruptly and calling Gene to meet him at New City. As he started downstairs he realized that he was still out of coffee at home.

CHAPTER 51

Nearly three more hours passed before they figured out what had happened. Walt and his men were taking some history from involved personnel when Ron and Gene arrived. Tom Bolling was there to assess the damage and loss and a good deal of activity was taking place to treat individuals wounded in the robbery.

What finally emerged was the story of how two men had kidnapped one of the nurses leaving the hospital after completing her shift at 11:00 PM. She had parked in the employee lot closest to the Loading dock and took a short-cut to her car by going down the back hallway and out the poorly lit loading dock. She was grabbed there and taken to a nearby car and placed in the back seat and gagged. One of the men sat with her and the other remained in the driver's seat. When a security vehicle took a swing through the lot, the nurse was forced to slump and the two men also dropped below the level of the seat so the car looked empty. She said the men said very little but they had sandwiches and water bottles and were prepared for a waiting period.

The nurse said the men took her out of the car around 3:00 AM. She saw the clock on the car dashboard as they were moving her out. They kept her gagged and re-entered the hospital through the loading dock. They explained what she was expected to do as they went down the back hallway to the rear door of the Pharmacy. They removed her gag and put her face up close to the eyehole. One man put a knife to her throat and the other stood out of sight to the side of the door.

As instructed she knocked on the door and told the person on the other side she needed some immediate medication for a ward patient.

Apparently she was recognized and the door was unlocked. The man at the side then kicked the door open and rushed inside. The nurse was also pulled inside and the door closed and re-locked by her captors.

When the door was kicked open it hit the night pharmacist in the face and he was lying on the floor with blood gushing from his nose. One of the kidnappers told her to tend to him and the other stepped to the edge of the nearby cabinets as the nighttime technician came into the area to see what the noise was all about. The man at the cabinets grabbed the technician by the collar and shoved the knife next to his throat and ordered him to take him to the narcotics. Apparently, there had been a delivery of narcotics that day that had not yet been completely inventoried.

The two men pulled large shoulder bags out of their clothing. The nurse said they looked like mail pouches. They quickly opened all the narcotic packages and emptied the contents into their bags. As they were finishing one of them went deeper into the pharmacy and came back with a bottle and a towel. The pharmacist was unconscious but the bleeding had stopped. The men grabbed the technician and put a towel over his face and poured chloroform on it. He kicked and struggled for a couple of tense minutes before finally slumping asleep. The two men laid the technician on the floor and turned him on his side. And then they put the towel on her face.

When she awoke about 20 minutes later according to the large wall clock above the door, she was bound with zip ties on both her hands and feet. The technician was already awake and was trying to get out of his ties. Together they were able to get a drawer open where he knew there were some scissors but it still took a long time for them to cut the ties. When she was freed she turned to helping the pharmacist and the technician called security.

When security arrived and assessed the damage they called the director and Tom Bolling who told them to alert the police. Bolling came over to Ron when the assessment of loss was almost completed. "Seems like they got several hundred doses of fentanyl, about a hundred vials of morphine and two cases of Demerol. This is a big haul."

Walt Matthews was right behind the chief of staff and said, "From what the nurse tells me this is the gang we're looking for. One of the guys that grabbed her was a guy that Scooter had tipped us off about, Froggie Isselson. If Froggie is still here, the rest of the gang is probably here, too."

Ron looked at the group and said, "And that raises the most important question of all: Why are they still here?"

CHAPTER 52

Walt Matthews believed he knew the answer to the question: 'why is the drug gang still in Cincinnati?'. In his opinion they were here to ply the stolen drugs into the street as quickly as they could and take the cash and head for another city. Accordingly, he left New City and marshaled his Drug Unit personnel to double-time on the streets, to find dealers and watch their movements, and track down these outsiders.

Ron and Gene, as non-participants in the Drug Unit, stayed at New City and by 9:00 AM were sitting in Tom Bolling's office and chewing on the same question, and none of them were as certain as Walt Matthews that they knew the answer.

"Maybe they want to distribute these drugs on the street and make a getaway but with all the heat right now they would take a beating on the price," Gene offered.

"I think that's right," Ron added. "I think there's something else going on. For them to stick their neck out of the street right now would be careless and they don't seem like careless people to me."

"Didn't you tell me there was a new development in the overdose business?" Tom asked.

"Yeah," Ron said. "I got that directly from Walt. He said there had been something like twice as many deaths from overdose this year. He said the biggest increase was in an elderly population, not street activity."

"But he still thinks the gang is going to get involved in the street traffic?" Gene took a long drag on his coffee and thought again how much better it was, this 'usual' of his, than what they got at the coffee shop.

"Yes," Ron answered the non-question. "He still sees the street as the major domain of drug dealers. This is his life. He's the expert."

Tom said, "But what if he's wrong? I mean, look at this the way an epidemiologist would. There's this ongoing base level of drug activity with a stable rate of overdoses occurring per unit time. Then two things happen about the same time. First there's a 'new gang' in the neighborhood, our 'sources', 'Scooter' for instance, tells us they are dealing drugs and doing well and then the second thing develops: a whole new population of 'users' that overdose. That population is, of course, the elderly. We would look at that sequence of events and say 'the second event is related to the first until proved otherwise'."

After a moment or two of reflection, Ron said, "That makes a whole lot of sense."

Gene nodded.

The agreement on this principal did not move them much farther down the track, however. Ron thought out loud, "If they are planning on marketing their haul from the pharmacy, and if they are not planning on doing it on the street, what are they going to do?"

Tom asked, reasonably. "Why do anything different from what they had been doing? Nobody seems to know what that is and if we're right it doesn't involve the street and it will involve elderly people."

"Even so, we don't know who those elderly people are and how they make contact."

Again Tom broke the ensuing silence. "Seems to me like another epidemiological question. "Who are the intended customers?" and I would ask "What is the common feature of those who overdosed and died?" Do we know that?"

"I don't," Ron said.

"Me either," Gene added.

"Well we all know one common factor," Tom said. "They all died. And medical personnel should be able to see if there's anything further that they all had in common. How can we get the records of known overdoses?"

"I'll bet that Walt has a list," Gene said quickly. "He won't mind us doing our thing."

"Well, he might not mind as long as we don't get in his way," Ron said remembering how Walt had shut down his BOLO on 'TJ' because it would possibly tip off the gang.

Tom was now leaning forward and ready for battle. "Look, you guys get the names of those people and I'll get their medical records for us to go through."

Ron agreed, "This won't get in Walt's way at all. He may welcome a second look at the problem."

Gene added as he stood and prepared to leave, "Tom, if you're right about this group being aimed at a whole new customer base, we may have the only chance to figure out who they are before the gang is long gone."

Tom nodded and added, "I'll have a War Room set up here as soon as you can get me some names."

CHAPTER 53

Walt was intrigued about the possibility of Tom's idea and told Ron to run with it. Walt and the Drug Unit didn't have the staff to cover both avenues and he was committed to covering the street. Further, he admitted the Drug Unit did not have the medical expertise that Tom was willing to add. Therefore it made all kinds of sense for Ron and Tom to head up the 'medical' investigation regarding the elderly deaths. Walt told his IT person to immediately turn to locating the names and pertinent information on the deaths and confirmed non-fatal overdoses in that age group and getting that to Ron.

Ron stopped in to discuss the new information and their plan with the Captain. Thorason sat quietly at his desk as Ron explained the reasoning behind he and Gene working out of the New City Hospital on a drug case rather than in their own office working a homicide. When Ron had finished his briefing, Thorason lowered his head for a moment and looked back at Ron from under his eyebrows.

Ron thought he was about to get The Look and braced himself. Instead Thorason looked up and smiled, in itself an unusual occurrence. Then he said, "I think you're right. Be fun to scoop the Drug Unit, too. Go do it."

Ron breathed a sigh and went to his desk to get necessary papers before heading to the hospital. He was relieved that Thor had agreed with their plan but he realized he had just heard Thor give a positive order for the first time in months. The 'Go do it' in Homicide was the equivalent of Jean Luc Picard saying, "Make it so." He called Gene to tell him of the decision and headed for New City.

Tom had commandeered one of the small IT training rooms to serve as a War Room. The head of the Information Technology division at New City had assigned a senior technician to set up individual workstations for them and to remain available for support. Each of them had a desk with two monitors, one networked to the others so they were all looking at the same screen and the other was connected to the Internet for their use in searching certain databases. Each of them also had a large area on an adjacent desktop available for any papers they were using. And, perhaps most important, when the detectives arrived, there was a fresh 'usual' sitting by their keyboard, courtesy of Nick via Tom Bolling's request.

"Man, I could do this more often!" Gene said happily.

"So we could. So we could," Ron agreed.

By 2:30 that afternoon, Walt's IT expert had provided them the names of the Cincinnati individuals who were known to have had opioid overdosing. There were 16 in the last three months; nine of these died. The major part of the afternoon and evening was devoted to reading what medical information Tom could obtain on these individuals. Some information came from Monique Song helping to obtain official death certificates on those who had died. Tom determined where the patients were seen with their overdose but that turned out to be the nearest hospital and not one where they might have received regular care. He was spending more time calling chiefs of staff at other hospitals in the area to enlist help in finding previous medical records and two other record clerks were helping him to compile the data. Ron was able to get the coroner's full report on most of the ones that died in an Emergency Department or unexpectedly at home.

Gene gathered the data to frame a big picture of the issue. According to health statistics, Cincinnati and Hamilton County had suffered the second highest rate of death from drug overdoses in both 2016 and 2017. And the incidence was not receding; in the last six months there were documented 251 overdoses of which 138 were fatal for a death rate in that subgroup of 55%. The granular specifics on those cases were available and that data showed what Walt had said: 16 of these cases involved patients over the age of 65, nine of whom had died. Three of those deaths occurred at home and became coroner's deaths because they were unexpected. Six deaths occurred across various Emergency Departments and also became coroner's cases. There were seven other cases identified as having an overdose that was non-fatal because of prompt treatment by first responders or the ED staff.

There were some reports of interviews with surviving patients or family members of those who died. The information was understandably muted but in essence came to the conclusion that the individual patient had 'probably taken too much of prescribed narcotic' and the case was not further examined. That information alone led Tom and Ron to an intense discussion.

"Why wouldn't those doctors or nurses ask more questions?" Ron wanted to know.

"Well, I can't be certain," Tom replied trying to sooth the issue, "but what they were told was this was an accident involving prescribed medication. And bear in mind they only saw one case. Only one of the EDs saw more than a single case."

"Still, this is unusual isn't it? Should they have been more inquisitive?"

"Maybe," Tom said, "but recall most of these cases came in during busy times in the ED. It probably looked rather cut-and-dried at a time when they had other patients to see and treat."

"OK. Maybe I'm just a little defensive."

"Really? What about?"

Gene broke in, "We had our own problems with wrong questions recently. Ron's just thinking back on that."

Tom looked at his friend and asked, "Want to explain?"

So, over the next half hour, Ron and Gene spilled the story of their questioning of Tom Whelan that was too pointed and short. Tom nodded at several points in the story and they fully expected him to interrupt. He let them finish, however, before commenting, "You've just been through what we have to teach every medical student."

"Really? What's that," Gene wanted to know.

" The first part is how you settled on Whelan to start with. You said it yourself: military, Special Ops, living in the area and had a limp.

Bingo. You jumped right to the final diagnosis. In medicine this is what we call 'early closure'. You have essentially closed off all the possibilities of your murderer being anyone other than Tom Whelan."

"Well, yeah. We see that in retrospect. On the investigation side, we call that profiling."

"So do the young doctors. But what we need, and you do too, is to be able to see that possibility prospectively. Because when you don't it leads to the next flaw: asking the wrong questions."

"To be fair, our questions weren't wrong."

"To be really fair, they weren't' right either, were they?"

"Well, we got around to it, finally."

"Even a blind hog . . ."

"Oh come on, Tom."

"Let me tell you a personal story. I'm the hero here so pay attention. I was doing an externship in a small town hospital between my junior and senior year with one of my classmates. In the middle of a quiet afternoon we get called to the Emergency area because a local man had just brought his father in comatose. Jim and I arrived at the same time and heard the man say, "My dad's had a heart attack." Jim was all over that, he wanted to be a cardiologist and he elbowed past me and said, "I'll take care of him." He then hustled the man on the ambulance gurney into the hospital for care, leaving me to talk to the son.

Thinking it important to get more information I asked, "Can you tell me about your father's heart attack?"

He said, "It's a heart attack, you know."

I said, "I understand. But what was it like?"

He said, "Who are you?"

I said, "One of the medical students here at the hospital."

He snickered, "Medical student, huh? Don't you know about heart attacks?"

I said, "Yes, of course. But I'd like to know more about your father's. What was it like?"

Then he got mad and shouted at the Emergency nurses, "What's with this guy? Don't they teach you anything? He had a heart attack! Just like has had several times before!"

I said, "What are those 'heart attacks' like?"

He said, "It was a heart attack! Just like all the others. He falls down and shakes all over and wets his pants. You know, a heart attack!"

Tom paused as the meaning of the story sank into Ron and Gene. Then he said, "Of course, he didn't have a heart attack. He had a grand mal epileptic seizure. I had a lot of fun with Jim about that one."

Ron took a deep breath and said, "Point taken. And back to this case, it seems we each have some interesting data but can't make heads or tails. I think we need to put it all together."

Ton quickly agreed, "sometimes some big thing jumps out when all the data are presented the right way."

CHAPTER 54

E ven using the computers and a clever 'merge' function, they didn't get their individual data on 251 cases into a spreadsheet for two hours. Gene knew more about manipulating the spreadsheet than Ron and Tom combined and he took over the responsibility to create several other individual spreadsheets from the master one where he sorted the items by various factors. Each of those sheets seemed not to have any definitive trend or commonality between cases.

Ron finally suggested that they weren't really interested in all the 251 cases anyway and that Gene should pull just those cases over age 65 for analysis. As he did so, Ron and Tom began to get more excited about the data. Finally, Gene created a table with only a few parameters that they all decided would likely be of help. Tom reasoned this way: "If in every one of these cases, fatal and not, the patient was taking a narcotic we should look for why that narcotic was prescribed."

Gene's chart provided only data on age, sex and outcome on the 16 cases in its first iteration. Tom immediately turned to his task of pulling information from hospital records for those 16 individuals. He was particularly interested in their latest hospital stay and the discharge diagnosis. As he was entering these data into Gene's table he added additional information on certain patients whose last medical encounter had been as an outpatient.

Ron and Gene looked at the final table and said, "That's it."

But Tom was not satisfied. He said, "Go ahead and study that if you want. I think there's something more here if I can get to it."

A half-hour later he said, "Bingo. I just didn't know where to look at first but here it is. I found the outpatient follow-up for these people. Every one of them was recommended for Physical Therapy. So I searched for the Therapy Notes and 'Bingo!' "

Ron said "I think you can only Bingo once per card. Tell us what you're talking about."

"Every one of these patients had a pain control problem associated with a diagnosis that often requires therapy to obtain maximum recovery. They were all given a small number of narcotic pills at discharge and started on therapy. Only one of those patients completed the prescribed therapy. And although I don't have the data I bet if we pulled their pharmacy records we would not find any refills on their prescriptions for narcotics!"

"Because our guys were getting to them somehow and selling them narcotics door-to-door." Gene was sure he had it.

"Makes sense but is it right?" Ron asked. "Is this early closure?"

"Actually it doesn't make sense," Tom said. ""Would you start buying narcotics from a door-to-door salesman? No, of course not. They have some other way of appealing to these patients."

He went on, "While it is true that all of these patients had a painful circumstance and were prescribed physical therapy, not all patients with such conditions are on this list."

"What's your point?" Ron asked, puzzled.

"If not everyone with a fracture or major surgery is on this list we must be missing another common denominator that identifies these patients out of the larger group."

"What could that be? I mean we already had 15-20 other parameters that we decided to take out of the table. Is there one of those we need to put back in?" Gene was ready for that if necessary.

Tom took a deep breath and said, "No, it's not something we have in their medical file. It's something we often forget. I think it's the payer information. Do either of you have the insurance information on these sixteen?" They did not.

But in another hour, they did. As the time approached 1:00 AM, Tom laid down his pencil and announced, "Bingo again. I changed cards. We got 'em!"

"What did you find?" Ron inquired from where he was laying his head on his arm.

"We don't even have to put these data in the table because they are all the same. Every last one of these patients was insured by the same insurance company."

"Who is it?" Gene asked.

"It's a relatively new company and I don't know much about them. They're called 'Licking River Health Insurance Company' and I know who can tell us all about them."

"Can he tell us later in the day?" Ron asked from his desk.

"Absolutely he can, he works for me," Tom said closing down his computer.

Gene saved all his data to a disc and then printed out the table they had focused on, minus the column identifying Licking River as the Insurer of each patient on the list.

Age	Sex	DX	IP/OP	Disch	Outcome	PT
67	F	Colles-R	OP	1-22	Died	Inc.
73	M	L hip fx	IP	1-25	Died	Inc.
76	M	CABG	OP	2-2		Inc.
81	F	Fx elbow	IP	3-2	Died	Inc.
69	F	L HIP FX	IP	3-20	Died	Inc.
72	F	Fx Humerus	IP	2-15	Died	Inc.

73	M	AAA	IP	2-28		Inc.
69	M	R ankle Fx	OP	3-22		Inc.
83	F	R femur Fx	IP	4-16	Died	Inc.
76	M	Fx elbow	OP	4-2	Died	Comp
75	F	CABG	IP	3-24		Inc.
83	M	L hip Fx	IP	4-15	Died	Inc.
67	F	Compr FX L2	IP	3-3		Inc.
69	F	Appendx	IP	2-29	Died	Inc.
72	M	Colles	OP	4-6		Inc.
70	F	Shoulder	IP	3-29		Inc.

CHAPTER 55

At 10:15 the next morning, Tom took Ron and Gene to the Business Office at New City and introduced them to Karl Breslinger, Chief Financial Officer for New City. Breslinger was a large man, at least six feet tall with a large chest and abdomen, dressed in a dark grey pinstriped three-piece suit complete with watch chain. His large face was intended to be in a neutral composition but the ends of his mouth naturally turned downward so he looked as if he were frowning at everything. He gestured his guests to sit at the rectangular table and he rolled his desk chair to joint them.

He turned to Tom and asked, "What's this about Licking River?"

Tom explained briefly that the detectives had identified several patients from New City and other hospitals that had been involved after their discharge in 'some kind of fraud' exercise and that the three of them had just recently discovered that the only common thread between these patients was Licking River.

Breslinger nodded solemnly and the corners of his mouth did not change. Tom used his hands to discourage Ron from jumping into the conversation and went on, "Since I didn't know much about the company but I did remember you telling me recently that they were new in the market, I thought you might tell me, or us, what you know about them?"

"Are you thinking they are dirty?" Breslinger asked, turning to Ron as he did.

"Actually, sir, we only just became aware of their presence in this case. It seemed to us that the common thread of this particular company in each of the victims, er, patients, was simply something we need to put in perspective. It may be nothing, it may be circumstantial, or it may be that the source of our case is linked to this company."

"I see." Still no change in the mouth.

"Anything you could tell us would be helpful, sir. We can always go directly to the company, probably could get a warrant for their files, and check with every one of their insured and things like that. But it would be really disruptive and take a long time. Tom, Dr. Bolling, suggested we could get a good idea of whether we need to pursue this angle further from your insight and expertise."

Tom realized he had never actually used either 'expertise' or 'insight' in referring to Karl Breslinger, just calling him a 'source'. But he smiled broadly at Karl and nodded sagely.

Breslinger looked at each of the men for a few seconds as they looked back with open expressions and guileless appearance.

"I know about your HIPAA laws against releasing personal health information," Breslinger finally said. "And in the financial world we have similar constraints against disclosures that have investment or brokerage implications. Insider trading and the like. Of course, what you are asking has nothing to do with investment does it?"

"No." Tom spoke up. "What the detectives are wondering is since this company only recently entered our market, how have they done and is there anything particularly interesting about their business model?"

"Business model is it, then?"

"Well, whatever it is that you might find 'interesting'. Sir." Gene added.

Breslinger used another pause, not as long this time and then his mouth corners went up. "I couldn't imagine what you wanted to know about these guys, Tom," he said. "If you want to know how they're doing, their business model and whether they have need to get in bed with some shady business, I can help you get over that thinking."

Licking River had started business in Hamilton County a little more than 14 years ago. The company was founded and initiated with funding from its two principals, both of whom had made significant money in the dot.com world and got out before the collapse. They have given speeches to the business community in the county about their reason for starting Licking River and it seemed to be a decent blend between community service and capitalism.

According to Breslinger, the principals at Licking River hired some bright young people with artificial intelligence background and spent over 16 months analyzing the public county and national health records to determine actual costs, within predictable ranges of less than a dollar, for a cohort of patients with a variety of common medical diagnoses and surgical procedures. Once the principals were satisfied their algorithms were accurate and stable, they launched the company with premiums that were substantially lower than that even of national companies. But the locally attractive part of the system, Breslinger had heard from patients themselves, was the ultra-friendly AI interface.

Almost everyone has had the experience of interacting with a digital interface and being routed to the wrong office, made to answer questions that were not of the caller's interest or being told that they needed several layers of identification in order to proceed. Licking River interface is entirely different in that each policy holder does a telephone interaction with the AI system during purchase and the system 'saves' for later identification purposes not just the number from which they call but also their voice modulation. The result is a seemingly personal greeting from 'Irene' a quick question to confirm identity and then the caller can speak almost anything they wish to get the system response.

According to Breslinger, the AI telephonic system at Licking River was based on thousands of interviews and focus groups and was capable of interpreting the caller's wishes from standard conversational English. Such a comfortable system coupled with the reasonable premiums had been successful over the last decade in slowing growing the company's enrollment. Further, the more enrollees that Licking River was covering the greater their pool of information about individuals and more accurately they could predict needed care and cost of that care. And they generally used that information to lower their premiums even more. According to the business community in Hamilton County, as best they can tell the principals continue to make money on volume and they pay their staff well.

When he finished his story, Breslinger leaned back with a real smile and asked, "Does that fit your picture?"

Tom was about to answer when Gene spoke up. "Well, it certainly could. All that computerization and use of algorithms creates an environment where an additional formula that pulls out certain patients or characteristics, like whether they need physical therapy, would easily go unnoticed." He aimed the latter part of this comment at Tom.

Tom nodded and said, "Thanks, Karl." He looked at Ron. "Anything else you think we should talk about?"

Ron looked quickly at Gene and then agreed, "No. I think this has been very helpful. Thank you for that information, Mr. Breslinger."

They stood and turned toward the door, Breslinger pushed his chair toward his desk. Gene stopped at the door and queried, "Who do you have your insurance with, Mr. Breslinger?"

"Licking River," was the prompt answer, accompanied by a full mouth grin.

CHAPTER 56

They took the time to swing by the Green Bean kiosk in the lobby to allow Nick to craft a 'usual' for each of them before they went back to Tom's office for another review of the 'knowns'. This time they focused on the drug business.

Gene started with, "It sure seems to me that the emphasis in the company to slice and dice their metadata would make it easy for there to be an unnoticed program that selects patient discharged with an order for physical therapy."

Tom agreed, "But that may not be the actual thing that is sought by the program."

"What would it be, then" Ron wanted to know. "I mean the common feature for all these patients was physical therapy, right?"

"Right," Tom agreed. "But just like not all surgical cases were in our list, not all patients referred for physical therapy were either."

"I don't follow."

"Remember, we are looking for some reason for this gang to select patients as candidates for narcotics. While physical therapy isn't pain-free most of the time patients are not looking for narcotic pain relief. I think this has more to do with conditions or procedures that create a small window of opportunity for narcotics to be of assistance. I think this set-up is identifying patients that need narcotics and getting to them right after discharge."

"That does make some sense," Ron noted. "But what made you think that?"

"First, I've prescribed a lot of physical therapy and followed patients during the course of their recovery. After a week or so, there is simply no need for narcotics. More important in this case, I noticed something else that's not on our table."

Gene said, "Oh no. Don't tell me that table needs re-doing."

"Oh no," Tom laughed. "But when you go check you'll see that these patients all quit their therapy, or at least stopped showing up for therapy, after only one or two sessions. Something convinced them to not go back. I'm guessing it was better pain relief."

"That actually makes very good sense, even for a Razorback," Ron grinned.

"What does that do for our understanding, though?" Gene probed.

"Just because it fits is no reason to stop looking for corroboration," Ron noted. "Tom, could you get us in to talk with some of these patients?"

"I had a thought about that earlier today on the drive in. I know a patient who is not on that list but who did stop his therapy. The therapists asked me about him. I'll ask him why he stopped."

"And we will go with you."

"Alright. But I don't want you doing the 'homicide thing' till we have this drug thing better nailed down."

"We're comfortable with you asking the medical questions. We just think we may need to ask some simple follow-up."

"If you think you can keep it simple, I'll go along with that."

Gene said, finishing his coffee, "Let Ron do it, then He's the most simple of us all."

Chapter 57

Once they had a handle on the process of the drug scam, it still took them two days and several interviews to get the entire story. When Tom and Ron believed they understood that satisfactorily, they gathered the other key players. Sitting in the conference room at precinct headquarters to hear the story and to decide on next steps were Captain Arne Thorason, Lieutenant Walter Matthews, Dr. Tom Bolling and detectives Ron Looney and Gene Novalchek.

Ron was the principal storyteller; he and Tom had gained the bulk of the initial information and Ron and Gene had filled in many of he details in subsequent interviews. A patient from New City that Tom knew personally initially sketched the story out. Tom had consulted on the man prior to his surgery and followed his course in the hospital. Tom had tried to see him during his rehabilitation in the clinic but the man had only shown up for the first session. When Tom and Ron visited him he admitted he had skipped the therapy sessions but insisted his knee replacement recovery was doing well and exhibited that by running up some stairs.

The man, almost 70 years old, explained that his life was fairly active and the rehabilitation schedule interfered with other activities he had planned so he got a set of instructions from the therapists and did his exercises at home in the evenings. Tom examined the wound and the joint flexibility and pronounced the recovery as good as expected after knee replacement.

Tom then brought up the subject of post-operative pain control and the man said he simply was not going to use opioids at all. He took some acetaminophen and some long-acting non-steroidal anti-inflammatory for a few days after coming home but nothing thereafter. The team thought this was a dead end and started making for the door when the man said, "That's why I told those research guys to leave me alone."

He told them how some 'researchers' from a pharmaceutical company had visited him at home after his first visit to physical therapy. These 'researchers' said they were working in conjunction with his insurance company to offer a new non-addicting opioid for pain control if he would agree. They said it would be at no cost to him except that they would need to have frequent visits to obtain information about how well the drug was working. The man told them, "Thanks but no, thanks," after explaining that he would not be taking any opioids at all.

He was able to describe the men generally but somewhat vaguely; it turned out they came to the door when he did not have his glasses on and his memory of their appearance was consequently blurry. Both were dressed in dark suits, one was thin with long hair and the other was larger and the suit did not seem to fit him well. The thin man did most of the talking. The large man appeared to be bald. They did not leave a card or a contact number.

Armed with this information, Tom and Ron decided to call on the spouse of one of the patients who had died of an overdose. This man seemed a little eager to talk to them about the events and said,

"It's about time someone showed up to get the full picture of this research project!"

Tom spent the next half hour slowly getting the man to give them the history from the first encounter with the 'researchers.' The same two men approached him and met with him and his wife, an 81-year-old woman who had taken a fall on their back steps and fractured her arm at the elbow. She had been seen and treated completely in the Emergency Department at one of the other local hospitals and given opioids for pain and scheduled for physical therapy Physicians in the ED told her that she might need surgery in the future if her arm bone ended up being shorter than it should be. The husband explained that the therapy was very difficult for her and they had decided to wait until she had healed before returning. He also said the 'researchers' thought that was a splendid idea.

They made the same pitch to him and the wife; the couple liked the idea of free medications and the wife was having a good deal of pain not completely relieved by the prescription medications she received at discharge.

The couple agreed to the 'research protocol', signed several forms for consent and non-disclosure. The 'researchers' explained the latter form as necessary for the company to provide the new medication for free. As in the previous setting, the thin man did most of the talking and the couple was given an initial trial bottle of pills and instructions.

The wife's fracture and fixation was in early March, the thin man visited the family weekly and when the pain increased he increased the dose of the medication. After three weeks, the husband said his wife spent most of her time sleeping and began to lose weight. Just over a week before the detectives came to call on him, the husband said his wife was shaking and demanding her medication sooner than prescribed. He told the thin man about this and was told that the company had decided to abandon the research and there would not be any more drugs.

This information devastated the couple, as their impression was the medication was highly successful in abolishing her pain; they wanted more of it. The thin man said all his stock was being inventoried for return to the company. The husband offered money for some of the remaining stock but the thin man said it was too risky. After some negotiation, the husband offered three thousand dollars for a cache of the medication and the thin man agreed. He gave the wife some that he had in his pocket and made an appointment to return.

This return visit, however, did not have the promised amount of drug involved. Again, the story of difficulty in manipulating the inventory was the answer and more money was promised. This time the husband said the money was dependent on the delivery, however. Two days later the wife took an overdose and was declared dead on arrival at the nearby hospital. The thin man never showed up again.

With this understanding of how the gang was distributing their drugs, Ron and Gene made additional visits to three more patients or survivors and found essentially the same story with minor details varying at each location depending upon the effect of the drugs and the response of the family. Essentially the story was as presented by the first man whose wife died from an overdose.

The 'researchers' appeared at the home of a patient recently operated on or who had a fracture. They appeared usually after the first outpatient visit to rehabilitation for physical therapy. They represented a chance for 'free' medication, improved pain control and shortened recovery time from their 'research'. Multiple forms were presented and signed. At least once, a trial dose of the 'research' medication was used to convince a reluctant couple to agree to the 'research.'

Weekly visits were made, drugs were supplied and more notes about condition were obtained. Sometime after the third week patients receiving the 'research' drug began to increase their use and to exhibit signs of withdrawal. At this time the 'research protocol' was declared discontinued, all 'too bad'. The addicted person and significant other beg and plead and occasionally demand to be able to continue to receive the drug. The situation and the 'inventory' are explained, the risk of taking drug is too high, the 'mark' suggests money to offset the risk and a larger amount of medication is provided for a considerable sum of money. Thereafter the 'patient' often overdoses and the researchers are seen no more.

"Diabolical," said Thor, shaking his head.

"Clever," amended Walt. "This keeps them off the street and away from using a distribution ring with many hands in the pie."

Tom spoke next, "Before you go giving them an award for innovation, be aware that they are likely still in operation. That's why they hit the New City Pharmacy. They have some more money out there in the suburbs they want to collect before they disappear."

Walt nodded and said, "We need a plan to find the homes they are visiting and grab these guys ASAP."

"I disagree," Ron interjected. "We have an idea where they will be visiting but we need to track them back to their headquarters. There's a big stash of drugs hidden away and I'm still trying to catch a killer."

Arne added, "The homicide investigation takes some precedence here. Walt, work with us and we can all win."

Walt's initial thought was to fight this position but, even as he realized he was outranked, he looked at Thor's face gathering into The Look and decided on the wiser choice.

"Acceptable," he said, "as long as my guys are in the hunt."

Thor nodded.

Tom pulled out a sheet of paper with names and addresses of patients he thought likely to be on the gang's list to approach.

CHAPTER 58

Two days later the Task Force was able to report good news. The initial plan involved setting up distant surveillance on four homes of individuals that met the criteria from the Table Gene had developed. Each home housed an individual with either recent surgery or a painful fracture who had begun physical therapy but had not continued. All were insured by Licking River.

No activity was detected on the first day at any site but the second day started off by a sighting of the 'research' team at 10:00 o'clock at one of he residences. The observation team identified the car the 'researchers were driving and cautiously followed it when the gang left that house.

The 'research' team visited two more houses that day. The observation team began to feel a little obvious and called for a relay after the second house. The new trail team followed the 'researchers' to the last visit of the day and then followed them from Concord Hills down I-75 and then west on I-275.

The 'research' car took a south turn onto State 4 and took an early exit heading for the Sports Tavern. When they turned in at the Tavern the observation team had to continue on past but were able to turn into the parking lot at the nearby Day Inn and pull out of sight.

"You think they're just here for lunch?" asked one of the trail team.

"Maybe," came the team leader's answer. "But it's early and they may be heading for another mark. Just sit and wait."

Forty minutes later the 'researchers' were on the move. Their car left the Tavern parking area and turned right on Glensprings Drive and then left into the Springdale community. The trail car followed at a safe distance and saw the 'researchers' park in front of a low rancher. One person, a average sized guy in a dark suits got out and opened the rear door. He removed a briefcase and headed to the front door. The trail team drove past the house and turned at the next corner.

The front passenger contacted Walt, "Hey boss, I think the bald guy we're looking for is sitting in the car here. I didn't get a clean look but I think he fits."

"Stay nearby. We got the Glensprings exit tapped."

"Roger that. We're moving so the car is visible."

"Cancel that. Do the watch on foot. I don't want them seeing you and if you can see them . . ."

"Roger. Don will watch from the corner."

The 'researcher' stayed only a few minutes before returning to the car and driving off; the trail car waited for Don to regain his seat and followed slightly more than a block behind, trailing them back the way they had come into Springfield. At Glensprings Drive the gang car turned east and then south on State 4.

Walt paged the trail car, "Hey we got Sonny on 'em down 4. You can break off. I think they're heading into the city so you could head for the office and wait for us to call."

"Roger that."

The 'research' car continued down State 4 and ultimately merged with Vine St. before joining I-75 southbound. Walt called several teams to be ready in case the gang tried to go west on I-74, but they continued on past Cincinnati State and south through Camp Washington.

On a hunch, Walt set up surveillance cars on Western Hill and they were in perfect position when the 'researchers' turned west there and a few miles later turned toward Rapid Run Park.

"I think they're heading for their camp," came from the trail car. Maintaining a decent distance, they followed the gang car and watched it turn off toward a large camper on the edge of the Park. The trail team turned off before passing the camper and proceeded on foot through some minimal brush to a position where they could see the men in the car get out and enter the camper. A few minutes later another man exited the camper and went to the trunk of the car. He opened it, reached in and took out what appeared to be a large backpack and returned to the camper.

"We got, 'em, boss," said the trail team leader. "I think the big boss is here, too."

"Stick right there and keep us up to speed on their movements. We've got more cars coming."

Within the next hour two more drug cars pulled up to the camper each carrying two 'researchers' in dark suits. Between their arrivals, however, the man who removed the backpack from a car trunk came out and drove away in on of the vehicles.

After things had quieted down around the camper for an hour, Walt and his other men arrived and joined the watchers.

"How many in there?" Walt asked.

"Six. I'm afraid the boss left. Nobody's come in or out in the last hour but there's been some kind of celebration going on."

"Tell me."

"They were singing and shouting one time then we heard someone say 'Shut up!'. They've been kinda quiet since then."

"How long?"

"Maybe twenty minutes."

"And no one else has come out?"

"Nope."

"Alright, we need to take this group down and we need to do it fast. We don't have any information about weapons but we have to think they got some and will use them."

Walt's right hand man said, "That camper doesn't have a back door, so we're going to have to hit the front door with a lot of force and get inside quickly."

"You all know how to do that," Walt said without any question in his voice. ""Let's get down there and in position. Three on each side of the door."

They crept down from their vantage point and quietly approached the camper in two groups of three, one from each end of the vehicle. Walt was in the group to the left of the door and was using hand signals to indicate strategy when the door handle started jiggling from the inside.

Walt signaled everyone to pin up against the side of the camper just as the door opened and flooded the area with light. One of the men stepped outside into lighted area and started fumbling with the zipper on his pants. Walt pushed the door to the camper closed and stepped behind the man who was trying to take a leak. Walt grabbed him around the throat and chocked off any sound, turning his right hip into the man and lifting him off his feet. The struggle was minimal and the man shortly slumped to the ground.

Walt bent over him to secure him with a pair of handcuffs, one to the right wrist and the other to the left foot. The smell of alcohol was strong on the man and Walt figured he would be out for the duration. Some quick hand signals and the regrouped drug unit opened the door to the camper and pushed inside.

There was no resistance. There were three men in the front area of the camper and all were too drunk to stand. They took more than a minute to realize that the entry of the drug unit was not their friend returning from outside. By then, they were handcuffed and asking each other, "Hey! What's going on here?"

Walt quickly cleared the rest of the camper and found the remaining two culprits passed out on the bed in the rear bedroom. A quick call for a wagon ended the escapade.

Chapter 59

T he bald man sat in the interrogation room, sweating profusely. The room was not overly hot; he was sweating from anxiety that bordered on fear. Ron and Gene had just informed him that they were preparing to charge him with murder in the case of Margaret Kuykendahl. They showed him her picture and he started sweating. Once they were convinced he knew her they had questioned him intently on where he might have met her and finally uncovered the fact that he met her that night of her death in TJ's apartment. He said she just walked through the room and that he had left the apartment soon thereafter and gone to his own place.

Did he have witnesses? Not actually. The whole idea of the drug gang's plan was to be unnoticeable if not invisible. He had no corroboration that he didn't follow Margaret to the campus and kill her. So, the detectives told him they would be charging him. When they left the room 'to draw up the papers', he began to panic.

Watching from the viewing room, Ron turned to Gene. "How long should we let him sweat? He must have already lost five or six pounds. We're gonna have to get him some water in there soon, whatever else we do."

Gene replied, "He's got a lot more water to lose before I get concerned about his health. We know this guy is a tough nut. Record of drug dealing and incarceration in four states, suspicion of battery and known instances of intimidation. He thought he could get a little sentence and live it off. When you brought up the murder charge he was suddenly facing something he didn't expect. I say give him some more time. Let's go get coffee."

When they returned, Ron brought the bald man a bottle of water. The detectives sat across the able from him and Gene opened the conversation with, "Anything more you want to tell us about you and Margaret at the apartment?"

"Hey, no. It wasn't me with her, it was TJ and her. She actually came there to see him."

"That's new information, Pokemon. Why didn't you mention that before?"

"Uh. I didn't know it was important until you said that about her being murdered."

"You mean you didn't know about that?"

Pokemon paused and considered his answer. "I might have heard about it," he finally managed.

"How did you 'hear about it' then?" Ron pressed. "And when was this information shared with you?"

"It was TJ that told me. That night at the apartment, she came in and saw our guns and all the money on the table and the Boss man didn't like that. He told TJ she had to go."

"Go?"

"He had to get rid of her. She couldn't be around to tell you guys about what we were doing."

"You're saying that the Boss gave an order to kill this girl and TJ then told you later that he had done it? Is that what you're saying, Pokemon?"

"Uh, well, yes. I didn't have nothing to do with her. She just walked past me and went in the bedroom. I left before she came out. TJ told me'n the Boss man that he took care of her back at the University. Showed us the newspaper article."

Ron looked at Gene who shook his head and quietly said, "But Pokemon, we don't have either TJ or your Boss Man. But we do have you. And that will give us a person to hang this murder charge on. Too bad."

"What you mean, too bad'? I told you, I ain't the guy. The Boss, he ordered it and TJ did it. By himself. Said he just did the neck twist thing." "What is TJ's name?"

"I don't know. I never met him 'til this job. He was just 'TJ'. That's all."

"Do you know where he's from?"

"Nothing. I don't know nothing."

"Do you know where he is? Right now?"

'No, man. I ain't seen him all day. He usually goes out to do the collections but he was late showing up today and the Boss sent us out to collect before he showed."

"But he was there, at the camper, today?"

"I don't know for sure. I didn't see him. Boss said he went out for pizza or something just before I got back."

"And you don't know his real name?"

"No. I told you that already."

"How about the Boss' name, then?"

"Oh no. No. He doesn't want that out. He's always just the Boss."

"OK, Pokemon. If we can't get either of the other two, it'll just have to be you. And from what our medical examiner told us, it will be Murder One. No self-defense or anything like that. Murder One."

"Wait, wait, wait a minute. What do you mean 'since we don't have either one of them'? What's that mean?"

"C'mon, Pokemon, you're a smart guy. You know exactly what that means. If we had TJ, we'd get him for the murder on your testimony. And if we had the Boss, probably we could get him for Murder as an accessory. But we don't have them, do we?" Gene stood up and, as if on signal, so did Ron. They turned to the door and Pokemon said quietly behind them.

"I might have an idea about his name?" "TJ?" Ron asked spinning around.

"No. The Boss. He once gave me a credit card to get a car."

CHAPTER 60

After that, it was all downhill. Ron put the Boss' name into the system and had him located on the basis of his credit card purchases within three hours. They approached the motel where he was hiding and the manager easily provided them the room number. They broke down the door and caught him asleep and were able to bring him in without a fuss. A pair of detectives stationed at the camper picked up two other 'researchers' the following morning. Walt and his men scoured the camper and found most of the stolen narcotics wedged in a variety of hiding places.

The ring was broken; various assistant district attorneys were paging through the pile of records and information that Tom Bolling and Ron gave them plus all the meticulous records found in the camper. Indictments were being drawn up against the Boss for narcotic dealing, handling dangerous substances without a license, assisting in an unattended death and other, previously not used charges. The major lieutenants in the drug ring were clearly identified as Jim 'Pokemon' Davidson and Dave, 'Froggie' Iselsson and TJ. Charges against them were also numerous and a charge of Murder One was placed *in absentia* against the mysterious "TJ" on the basis of corroboration testimony taken from the Boss and the other lieutenants, including testimony that this "TJ" did volunteer to them that he had killed Margaret Kuykendahl prior to that news showing up in the newspaper.

The 'research project' was closed. All the currently involved individuals were contacted and provided access to drug addiction programs; two required hospitalization for withdrawal but there were no further deaths.

For a reason known only to him, Tom Bolling called the newspaper reporter, Daniel Edderman, and gave him an exclusive interview on the inner working of the team that broke the mystery of how the drugs were being distributed. Edderman was skeptical of the unanticipated contact and access to information.

"What's this all about?" he asked Tom at their first meeting.

"There are several people who did excellent work, over and beyond, to help the police crack this case. I imagine if you don't get that story and print it, it will never come out."

"And, of course, that includes mentioning you."

"Actually, I prefer that you keep my name out of any story. Your source will be: an well-placed individual at New City."

"I don't get it. What's in it for you, then?"

"Well, for one I'll see that the folks here who helped us with the computer work get recognized. Two, it will be a nice thing for the police to get recognition for a really great piece of work, especially now that your front page is running stories about police brutality."

"So, this is a political piece, then? Right, doc?"

"It is not and if you are not interested in getting a story unless you have dug it out from under a rock, we can just say never mind."

"No, no, no. I just don't see the secondary gain for you."

"Trust me. I'll be very happy with the truth being out there. You were a good guy in our previous dealings. Against your instincts probably, but you did the right thing and you got a good inside scoop on the story, didn't you?"

"Yeah but I think I had you guys by the short hairs and you had to give it to me."

"Do you really think that the degree and amount of detail we got you on that case came from us unwillingly and only because you had the leverage?"

"Well, yeah. I did. Isn't that true?"

"Not a bit, son. You will find that Detective Ron Looney and I are a pair of basic straight shooters. One or the other of us may withhold information from you during a case because it's necessary. But we won't do that afterward. I would think you might want to cultivate a good relationship with us. Here we are making what we think of as the first move. Are you in? Or should we find another reporter?"

After a brief pause, Edderman picked up his pad and pen and asked, "Where did this all begin?"

CHAPTER 61

In spite of the spring weather, the air was cool and somewhat more so in the shade of the large trees shadowing the Looney's patio. Ron invited Tom over for a beer after work so they could share memories and provide some feedback on issues only one of them might know.

They were on their second beer and had already discussed what each of them knew about the gang's mode of operations. They would slide into a town, assess the drug culture, and use their contact in the insurance company to get names of some possible targets. They didn't depend on there being a robovan full of drugs but were ready and able to hack that system and send the truck to their storage place. Otherwise, they depended on bringing a van through the Mexican border near Weslaco where they knew the system of drug sniffing dogs could be thwarted by covering the drug packets with cilantro and cayenne powder. With their supply safe in a storage bin, they began the faux research proposal by going to the homes of the recently treated and discharged patients with narcotic prescriptions. They counted on the fact that physician's generally under treated pain and the patients would be having significant reason to try the 'research protocol' on their second or third day home. Generally they chose upscale addresses reasoning that such persons as lived there would be less tolerant of pain and have more resources to keep the drug flowing when it came time for the 'protocol' to end.

According to the Boss, the addition of "TJ", who remained at large, to the team was not part of the original plan but he maneuvered his way into the upper ranks of the gang and had the skill and personality to persuade potential participants to join the 'study'.

Tom interjected at this point in the recitation, "I bet he's a true sociopath. They can lie about anything, including whether your mother loves you, and make it believable."

"He's definitely sociopathic," Ron agreed. "He killed a perfectly innocent young woman for almost no reason at all. And he's getting away with it."

Ron picked up the story to give Tom an insiders view of the drug hideout in the camper in Rapid Run Park. There were six gang members celebrating in the small camper when the drug squad approached. One guy came out to pee and was taken without a fuss. And, when the drug unit rushed the gang inside they found everyone drunk or high and unarmed. Ron said that Walt told him he had never had a bust go so well and end without virtually any violence or danger. There was that one gang member who got his nose broken but everyone agreed that was his own fault.

Tom indicated a need for the third beer of the six-pack of OTR he had brought. When Ron returned to the patio, Tom was stretching his back and walking the perimeter. He decided to tell the details of his discussion and 'interview' with Daniel Edderman standing up.

"He was pretty suspicious about talking to me at all."

"Cops and newspaper guys are always suspicious. Did he say he didn't trust you without some inside information that he could check?"

"No."

"See, we do that a lot. Cuts down on the confabulation of some street junkie who thinks he's got the inside track on a big deal coming down."

"Nope. He didn't ask for anything like that. But he did pound the question of what I would get out of him writing an article."

"And what did you tell him?"

"Pretty straightforward. I told him there were some folks who did yeoman's work in helping us break the code. People like our IT guy, for instance. And they should get a little applause."

"How'd he take it?"

"Skeptical. I also insisted he not quote me or mention anything about my part in the operation. Told him he could mention he had a highly placed source at New City."

"Ate that up, I bet."

"Well, it started the ball rolling. After that we talked for about an hour. I didn't give him any names of police involved. Told him I didn't know them. When I described the all-nighter running through the charts to find the common thread, he took copious notes and asked a lot of questions."

"Taking notes, huh? I would of thought he'd be a digital guy. Handheld recorder and all that."

"Oh, yeah, he was recording everything. And he was taking notes."

"Well, maybe he'll stay off our backs if this ever happens again." Ron did not sound like he believed what he had just said.

"Well, I think we may just have found someone to give us a good listen in the middle of a crisis and a fair story at the end." "We'll see. I'm still bummed that we can't get this "TJ" guy. It's pretty likely that he's split for sure now. There's no operation, no chance for money, no drugs to peddle. And Gene and I are out a murderer."

"I understand. What do you know about him?

"I've told you everything. He can wear a suit and sound persuasive. Sociopath. Prefers to wear chinos with an old Army jacket. And he is involved up to his eyebrows in drug trafficking."

"That's it?"

"In my book, yes."

"I think you may be missing one little detail about him and his habits," Tom said, finishing his beer and indicating he was about to go home.

"Yeah? What's that?" Ron asked, leaning back in his patio chair.

"Seems to me that almost every time we heard anything specific about him, it involved pizza," Tom said.

CHAPTER 62

This time they met at the Bolling's. Ron had called Tom and asked if he and Meg could bring pizza over to celebrate. When Tom asked about what they were celebrating, Ron had answered, "Oh, you know, Meg being back home. New granddaughter in our family. Lots of stuff."

Meg's return was more than a week previous as Tom knew, but he accepted these reasons because he wanted to see Ron again and also because he really liked pizza. He insisted that at least half of one pie was just pepperoni, his favorite. Ron complied with that request and arrived with two pies hot out of the oven.

"What's this deal with you and pepperoni pizza?" he asked as Tom checked the boxes contents.

"Goes way back," was the short answer.

"Can we hear about it?"

"At the table."

As the salad was being passed around Ron brought the subject up again. "Why are you so stuck on pepperoni? I thought you had more of a sense of adventure and would at least try sausage."

"It has nothing to do with adventure; pizza has a long and abiding presence in my history and initially it was always, and only, pepperoni."

"What's the story?" Susan got up to go get more drinks and said, "This could be a very long story."

"All right," Tom countered. "I'll make it short but it may not have the punch of the longer one."

"Go," Meg said grabbing a second slice of pizza.

"I left small town Arkansas at 18 and went to Gainesville for college. I didn't know anyone there but I settled in with a group of guys who were pre-med. We started studying together as freshmen and continued that for four years. During that period we studied together we sometimes had to move around because of the part-time job one or more of us had. One guy was a phlebotomist at a local hospital and was on call to draw blood all night. So we would go to the hospital and study together in the laboratory conference room. Another guy spent a year as a driver for a funeral home. He had quarters there at the home and we studied there even if he got a call and had to dress up in a suit and go out to pick up a body."

Ron raised his hand and looked at Susan. "Is this the bona fide short story?"

Susan laughed and said, "You don't have time for the long story. Stick with him. This is the slow windup but the fast pitch is just about to fly."

"No story-teller is revered in his own household," Tom retorted.

Ron pushed, "Lots of studying, Different places, we got that. Go on."

"The point is we almost always had pepperoni pizza while we were studying. I'm not sure there was any other kind of pizza at the time. Pepperoni pizza and frosty Coke-Cola. The memory is burned in. Even when I try another kind of pizza, everything falls short of those golden days."

"Aww. Now you're gonna make me cry," Ron said wiping a fake tear.

Susan interjected, "The long story has some really great parts, by the way. Things that went on in those odd study places."

Everyone paid attention to their own slice for the next few moments and then Susan asked Meg about the new grandbaby and that discussion went on without input from the men for the next 15 minutes.

When the pies were finished and coffee was being served Meg looked at Ron and said, "Are you going to tell them or should I?"

Tom and Susan both leaned forward and looked at Ron. He took his time wiping his mouth with a napkin and carefully placing the napkin next to his plate.

"C'mon," Tom said. "Are you pregnant?"

"Oh, man! No. We're thankfully quite beyond that kind of surprise."

"Well, what's the news, then?"

Ron sat up straight in his chair, looked at Tom and said, "I got him."

Susan asked, "Who?"

Tom said, "Really? How?"

Ron nodded to Tom and said, "It was something you said that keyed me in. You mentioned how TJ was always involved with pizza. He had it with Margaret, he missed the shoot-out at the storage unit because he was getting a pizza, he wasn't at the camper because he was . . ."

"Getting a pizza!" Tom finished for him.

"So I took the picture we had of him and started going to all the pizza shops in the metro area. Do you have any idea how many there are?"

"Probably somewhere between one and two gazillion, I'd guess."

"Slightly more, I think. But I found one out in Madeira where the delivery boy recognized his face. Couldn't remember the address though and I had to stake out the place for three days before he ordered another one."

"I take it you found him at home."

"We did. I called for some support and two of the guys went around to the back porch and strung some wire across the steps."

"Why?"

Meg joined the conversation and asked Tom if he watched any of the crime and detective stories on television.

"Well, yes. I can't stand watching the medical shows, though," he answered.

"Why not?"

"The treatments they propose are often just plain silly and the operating room drama is unreasonable."

"Well, detective Looney has a similar complaint about cop movies. Someone goes on a search for an armed and dangerous criminal and spots the dastard about a block away. The cop then pulls his weapon and shouts the criminal's name and starts running toward him."

Ron explained, "I presume the plot is a little thin and this way they can shoot a dramatic seven minute chase scene to fill in the time. So, before we go charging in to this house, we set a little trap if the perp tries to run. And, by the way, he did try to run."

Ron enjoyed telling this part of the story. "We bracketed the door before the pizza kid knocked. He probably thought we were television cops. As soon as he saw us outside the front door, he ran for the back door. And did the nicest head over heels I've ever seen an adult do. Guys in the back had him all cuffed and ready to go when Gene and I got out there,

"Did he confess?"

"No. But we have both Pokemon and the Boss telling the same story. He's indicted and we've got the proof. The ADA is tickled with the case."

"Well, congratulations. That's a big win for you. By the way, I have two questions for you. What does the 'T.J' stand for?"

"His real name. Teddy Jessup."

"And what did you do with the pizza?"

"I paid the kid for it and everybody involved in the takedown got piece."

ACKNOWLEDGEMENTS

I want to thank my wife and children for their encouragement during this writing process. Their feedback, support, and encouragement were positive factors in me finishing the original manuscript.

I also want to recognize Elle Murray for her faithful and frequent efforts to clean up the manuscript and to assist me in getting to the right place in decisions about format, artistry, and pagination.

Any errors that escaped these screening activities are mine alone.

Galen Barbour
Alexandria, Virginia
January 2023

Want more medical murder mystery?
Turn the page for an excerpt from the next book in the Ron
Looney series

The director of research at New City is brutally murdered; Ron Looney and Gene Novalchek are assigned the case. The obvious suspect is a surgeon-researcher who just lost his research funding and is now missing along with both technicians in his lab. More murders occur, killings with surgical precision, and Tom Bolling, chief of staff at New City, has to deal with a hospital administrator that does not appreciate academic medicine and a nursing executive who sees physicians not appreciating nurses for their knowledge and skill. The detectives cannot track the elusive surgeon until a late development forces them to change their thinking about the timeline and they become involved in a frantic race to prevent another murder

Sunset and dusk had come and passed into the growing gray of the evening. A brisk breeze from the northwest carried a slight chill and made the early Spring air feel heavier than usual. The parking area was poorly lit and contained only a few scattered vehicles. The man walking toward his car seemed tired, his steps were slow, and he did not raise his head as if he were watching every step. He was wearing blue scrubs and Velcro closured athletic shoes. When he reached the vehicle, he pulled his keys from the pocket of the short jacket he was wearing, opened the door, and plopped down heavily on the driver's seat. After a deep sigh, he pulled the door closed, leaned forward, and started the car but then put both hands atop the steering wheel and leaned his head on his hands.

After a few seconds, he sat up and let out another sigh, and leaned back in his seat. He was briefly aware of movement in the rear seat before a noose of some material was quickly placed over his head, shoved down to his throat, and pulled tight around his neck. His hands immediately went to his neck and discovered it caught in a heavy leather belt; before he could make a serious attempt at fighting the snare, he heard a somewhat familiar voice whispering harshly in his right ear.

"Calm down. Don't make sudden moves."

The driver was able to squeak out a minimal response.

"What you want?"

"Later. Don't talk. I have this belt where I can cut off all air and blood flow in less than a second. If you make any attempt to signal someone for help, I'll pull it tight. Do you understand?"

The driver nodded and tried to see his attacker in the rearview mirror but found it turned upward and of no use.

"We're going to take a little ride."

"Where?" came the gasping question.

"Never mind. I'll direct you. Let's go. Turn right out of the parking area. Go right at the next light," the whisperer responded.